I'M NOT TO GOSSIP

Tales from a small village

By
Kelvin Brown

MAPLE
PUBLISHERS

I'M NOT ONE TO GOSSIP: Tales from a small village

Author: Kelvin Brown

Copyright © Kelvin Brown (2023)

The right of Kelvin Brown to be identified as author of this work has been asserted by the author in accordance with section 77 and 78 of the Copyright, Designs and Patents Act 1988.

First published in 2023.

ISBN 978-1-83538-093-2 (Paperback)
978-1-83538-094-9 (E-Book)

Book Cover Design and Layout by:
White Magic Studios
www.whitemagicstudios.co.uk

Published by:
Maple Publishers
Fairbourne Drive, Atterbury,
Milton Keynes,
MK10 9RG, UK
www.maplepublishers.com

A CIP catalogue record for this title is available from the British Library.

All rights reserved. No part of this book may be reproduced or translated by any form or by any means, electronic or mechanical, including photocopying, recording or by any information storage and retrieval system without written permission from the author.

The views expressed in this work are solely those of the author and do not reflect the opinions of publishers, and the publisher hereby disclaims any responsibility for them.

Foreword

Nothing ever happens in Little Bardon, probably even less than in Great Bardon, a mile away on the road to Malbury, itself the nearest thing to a town in these parts.

Mrs Gill at the post office is always keen to inform visitors: "Nothing ever happens here," and Mrs Barnes, who was queen of the bakery for countless years until arthritis forced retirement, and is now a leading light in the WI, will tell any casual enquirer: "We ain't even got a proper bus service. What a place to live."

But Iris the postwoman always hints that there is more going on behind closed curtains than it is good to know; but, as she says: "You know me, I'm not one to gossip."

There have been moments of excitement, of course, like the time the King's Head ran out of pork scratchings and the pub's discerning gourmets who were lined up along the bar with their pints of Old Todger had to switch to cheese and onion crisps and pickled eggs for an evening.

Oh yes, and there was the excitement of the marrow growing competition, and the time the vicar raised eyebrows when he appeared in the pub with a woman on his arm!

There are places to visit, of course, like St Stephen's Church, the Union Chapel, Moss and Lumley's general store, the bakery and the post office. The sea wall, with its two concrete pillboxes left over from the war, and abundance of bird life, is only a couple of fields away and, most importantly for characters like Norman, Dennis, Sid, tuneless crooner Fred and Fred's son, Young Fred, there is the King's Head.

Most of village life seems to revolve around the King's Head, presided over by affable landlord Charlie and barmaid Peggy, who always seems to be called 'Peggy love' by the faithful public bar regulars, whose usual order is "pint of Old Todger and a bag of scratchings, please, Peggy love."

This is as exciting as it gets in Little Bardon...or is it?

Contents

Chapter 1 – Troubles With A Mobility Scooter 6

Chapter 2 – The Impeccable Mr Gudgeon 10

Chapter 3 – The Crime Wave 15

Chapter 4 – The Mysterious Colonel Crawford 20

Chapter 5 – Miss Meacham's Cat 26

Chapter 6 – Walter Woolacombe's Big Trip 32

Chapter 7 – The Marrow 36

Chapter 8 – Old Morton 42

Chapter 9 – The Sadness of Miss Day 46

Chapter 10 – Nozzer 51

Chapter 11 – The Walking Lady 56

Chapter 12 – Ghostly Goings-On 63

Chapter 13 – Good Old Percy 67

Chapter 14 – The Romany 71

Chapter 15 – Mayday Mayhem 76

Chapter 16 – A Night Best Forgotten 83

Chapter 17 – The Woo-Woo Club 87

Chapter 18 – History Bites Back 91

Chapter 19 – The Tin Man 96

Chapter 20 – The Last Cowboy 100

Chapter 21 – Fitness Fiasco 105

Chapter 22 – Carnival Day 110

Chapter 23 – Sorry, Auntie Gladys 115

Chapter 24 – Rumours 119

Chapter 25 – Sisters, Sisters 124

Chapter 26 – The Beach 128

Chapter 27 – The Beano 132

Chapter 28 – Cor, That's A Lovely Drop 137

Chapter 29 – She's Behind You 141

Chapter 30 – Let's Have A Party 147

Chapter 31 – It's Just Not Cricket 152

Chapter 32 – An Unlikely Hero 157

Chapter 1
Troubles With A Mobility Scooter

"Sid, Sid, come and give us a hand. I need a bit o' help here." Sid put his half-finished pint down on the King's Head's well-polished bar and shouted back: "Leave it outside, you daft sod. We don't want that in here."

"I'm not leaving it outside. It might get nicked," Joe shouted back. So Sid, Norman and Young Fred trooped outside and weighed up Joe's problem.

Joe had recently become the proud owner of a mobility scooter, a machine variously described by patrons of the King's Head over recent days as "well knackered" and "a heap of junk." Joe, of course, wasn't having any of that, he was adamant that it was a very good purchase, even if it did look as if it had already enjoyed its best days.

"And you can take that thing outside," said Peggy the barmaid, after the rescuing trio had manhandled it through the door to the public bar. "How many times do I have to tell you, you can't bring that horrible dirty thing in here?"

"Don't talk about Joe like that," said Young Fred.

"Very funny. But, Peggy love, it'll get nicked if I leave it outside," said Joe, with a sorrowful look. "Who in their right mind is going to steal that thing? Get it out," she snapped back. And so, Joe's pride and joy was manhandled back through the door, at the cost of some choice language from Sid and Norman and a scuffed knuckle for Young Fred.

And there it stood, outside the door, while Joe joined his brother Sid and the other regulars for a pint, and then another, and another, and so on until he could stand only with the assistance of a bar stool. It was Sid's birthday, after all, so it was only right that they all enjoyed the celebration.

And what a celebration it was, with Joe, Sid, Norman and Young Fred joined by Dennis and Fred senior - Young Fred's father and possessor of a very loud and tuneless singing voice. Despite Peggy's best efforts to stop him, an inebriated Fred broke into 'The Wild Rover' and only stopped when he stumbled backwards and spilt the remains of his pint down the front of his second best shirt.

And so the evening progressed, with the birthday celebrants gradually succumbing to the stupefying effects of the pints of Old Todger that were passed over the bar with a remarkable regularity. But sadly for those village stalwarts, all good things have to come to an end.

"Come on you lucky lads, haven't you got homes to go to?" called out a weary Peggy from behind the bar. There were a few attempts to sweet-talk another pint, but Peggy was having none of it; she had called Last Orders ten minutes ago, and Pc Nicholls had a habit of dropping by late on a Friday night to make sure glasses had been emptied.

"I don't know why you need that scooter, you only live 100 yards away and you walk as well as the rest of us," chided Norman, as they all stumbled out into the night air. "If the bobby catches you on it tonight, you'll be in trouble."

Not so, argued Joe in a rather incoherent way. How could he lose a driving licence he no longer had?

And anyway, he had skills he doubted any of his drinking pals possessed: he could ride it standing up and one-handed, and he would demonstrate those very skills to his disbelieving audience. But, the truth is, Joe was having a great problem standing at all, let alone riding a mobility scooter standing up and one-handed.

Joe was adamant that he was going to show what a clever and competent scooter rider he was, and no amount of argument from his staggering and stumbling friends would persuade him otherwise. In fact, their slurred attempts to discourage him made him even more determined to demonstrate his prowess.

So the mobility scooter was pushed into the King's Head car park and Joe was duly helped aboard, although with some difficulty. Norman fell over in the process, and Sid fell on top of him as he tried to help him up. Young Fred threw up in a flower pot and Fred senior broke into 'The Wild Rover' again, just as tunelessly as before.

"Hang on, let's get him started, see what he can do," said Dennis, the least intoxicated member of the party, and with that Joe took off across the car park at a giddying three or four miles an hour. "Turn," shouted Dennis. "Turn, turn," echoed Young Fred. But it fell on deaf ears.

They managed to retrieve the scooter from the grass strip at the side of the car park, and retrieved Joe from the fuchsia bush, and there the little adventure might have ended had it not been for Sid and Norman arguing over which of them was the better scooter rider - the scooter, of course, which neither had ridden before.

"Do you remember my old motorbike?" said Sid. "I rode that old BSA for years, and only got rid of it because of that night I put it in the ditch after the darts team's Christmas do and bent the forks."

There were nods of agreement from several quarters. They did indeed remember, but they remembered it as rather more than simply bending the front forks. They remembered it as a blind-drunk Sid being helped on to his motorbike outside the pub, riding off and being found in the ditch by a helpful policeman who arranged a bed for the night courtesy of the constabulary, and who testified in court that Sid had been three times over the drink-drive limit. Losing his licence for a year had been a great incentive to sell the badly damaged motorbike.

It was decided that Norman should be the first to show off his skill, and he was duly helped aboard, albeit seated instead of standing, and two-handed. He set off at a slow walking pace and made it half way round the car park before stopping to be sick.

"Let me show you how it's done," said Sid. "This brings back some memories." There were some in the party who swore afterwards that they saw the hint of a tear in Sid's eye, as nostalgia got the better of him. But this was no time to be dreaming of those heady BSA days, this was a time for action.

And that, in a nutshell, is how Sid came to end up in the King's Head's ornamental fish pond, together with Joe's pride and joy. He set off in good fashion, but unfortunately forgot to steer. Young Fred raced after him shouting "Stop, you daft old sod," but his cries fell on deaf and somewhat befuddled ears.

Young Fred was first on the scene, and bravely stood watching as Sid did his best to drag himself out of the pond, but his efforts were thwarted by an excess of beer that prevented co-ordination of movement.

The rescue party stumbled its way across the car park, amid hoots of laughter and Fred senior's rendition of 'What shall we do with a drunken sailor?' "It's not funny," said Sid, now standing, albeit with a certain swaying action, in knee-deep water. "Give me a hand."

They were doing that when a white Ford Focus with fetching stripes down each side, drove into the car park and Pc Nicholls got out. "What on earth are you lot up to? I thought it was a gang of hooligans. Go home, go to bed and hope Charlie the landlord doesn't sue you for damages."

Charlie didn't, but he did pin up a print of the picture Young Fred had the presence of mind to take on his phone, of dripping wet Sid up to his knees in water, next to the sorry-looking semi-submerged scooter. "That's what you call a good night," said Fred senior, with more than a little understatement.

Chapter 2

The Impeccable Mr Gudgeon

Little Bardon had never before seen anyone quite so daintily perfect as the impeccable Mr Gudgeon.

In another age he may well have been called a dandy, but in this one was called a number of things - none of them dandy, and mostly behind his back - which were not always very nice.

Mr Gudgeon was, quite simply, always perfectly presented, from the top of his immaculately coiffured head to the toes of his impossibly shiny shoes.

Some unkind souls described him as effeminate; in the pub they mumbled that "he must bat for the other side." But no-one knew, because no-one in the village ever got close to Mr Gudgeon.

Except Mrs Overend, that is, and the two formed the most unlikely alliance; he in his sharply pressed cavalry twills, blazer and cravat, she in a baggy tracksuit that desperately needed to see the inside of a washing machine.

Mr Gudgeon was Mrs Overend's lodger. He moved in with her and her collection of dogs, cats and assorted back garden menagerie when he arrived in the village a few weeks ago.

Any new face in the village provides a brief topic to add to the list of subjects from growing marrows to running the country that are chewed over nightly in the public bar of the King's Head and debated earnestly by the gaggle of wise women who pick over the choicest cuts of gossip at the WI market in the village hall every Thursday.

After the usual speculation about where newcomers come from, how much they might earn and where they spend their holidays, the unelected village elders move on to the next hot topic.

At least, that was always the way it worked before Mr Gudgeon stepped out of the taxi from the station outside Mrs Overend's council semi and picked his way over the broken rabbit hutch, discarded cardboard boxes and up-ended plant pots that formed a guard of honour to her front door.

For a village used to gruff farmhands in muddy boots and haughty women in 4x4s who smell of horses and Labradors, Mr Gudgeon was a revelation: a real live gentleman who was always immaculately dressed and who bade the village ladies good morning and wished them a good day.

He would raise his hat, then walk on quickly with strides so short that his legs appeared to be moving at twice the speed of those he passed and, because each foot moved at ninety degrees to its neighbour, he resembled a small, glossy duck hurrying down to the pond.

Mr Gudgeon was occasionally seen in the village with Mrs Overend; he immaculately turned out, trotting along on his short little steps, she lumbering along beside him, with tousled hair and dragged-through-a-hedge fashion sense.

They were a strange combination, and it was always a matter of great speculation as to why Mr Gudgeon had chosen Mrs Overend's chaotic domain for his lodgings.

Mrs Overend was a kindly soul, of course, and no-one in the village had ever had a bad word for her in the 30 years she had lived there, but she was hardly the sort of hostess one would have expected Mr Gudgeon to have chosen. If there were ever two sartorial opposites, it was surely Mrs Overend and her lodger.

Mr Gudgeon made great inroads into the hearts of the village ladies, with his charm and ready smile, but he never exchanged more than a few words, and hurried on when it looked as if a conversation might develop.

"He's a right gent, that Mr Gudgeon. Makes a nice change to meet someone as polite as he is, but have you noticed how he's always in a hurry," said Mrs Davis one day to Iris the postwoman.

"Not for me to divulge anything, of course, not in my job, but he gets a lot of posh-looking letters," said Iris, who would tell anyone who would listen that she was not one to gossip. "I don't know who they're from, of course, but some of them are in very expensive envelopes indeed, if you get my meaning."

Mrs Davis didn't get her meaning, if indeed there were a meaning, and nor did any of the other village sages who Iris casually told that day, with her usual rejoinder of "You know me, I'm not one to gossip."

Mr Gudgeon's postal deliveries became a matter of great conjecture among the herd of highly proficient inquisitors who passed as the ladies of the WI, when they met on the first Tuesday of the month, and St Stephen's Mothers' Union - largely the same - when they had their monthly get-together three days later.

Iris the postwoman's revelation that Mr Gudgeon received posh-looking mail was enough to put them into a feeding frenzy; the problem was that they knew nothing else about the poor man, and overtures made to Mrs Overend in the hope of eliciting information about her lodger were always ignored or rebuffed.

In the week that followed, he became, variously, a retired actor (but that was dismissed because no-one could remember ever seeing him on TV), an MI5 agent (but Mrs Gill from the post office said that was too stupid for words) and a host of other equally unlikely heroes.

Despite the most imaginative guesswork, no-one knew a thing about Mr Gudgeon's background - and they never would if Mrs Ferguson hadn't picked up an old copy of Country Life while waiting for her six-monthly check-up with the dentist in Malbury. She was so excited by what she read that she had the greatest difficulty keeping her mouth immobile while Dr Yates poked around inside.

She had barely cleared his doorstep before her trembling voice was imparting her information to Mrs Davis via the mobile phone that she usually had a problem working but which, today, necessity helped her to master.

Mrs Davis knew full well what she must do. The moment Mrs Ferguson said: "Must go, here comes the bus," she swung in to full gossiping mode, and soon had the village phone lines buzzing as the news about Mr Gudgeon spread from one wise old head to the next.

Retirement had not come easily to Mr Gudgeon. After 42 years as butler to Lord Ranchester, he knew it would not be easy to adjust to any other life, but he knew that he must, which is how he ended up in the village, residing in the chaos that Mrs Overend called home.

For an obsessively private man, it came as a terrible shock to Mr Gudgeon to discover that his former life was now village property, to be discussed in imaginative depth every time two or more of the gossiping fraternity met. It was little consolation to him to know that he was now held in even higher esteem among them; he would simply have preferred to be left in peaceful anonymity.

"I am sorry, dear lady, but I really could never even contemplate giving a talk to the Women's Institute on my professional life. Etiquette would never allow it," he told Mrs Davis when she asked. "Please pass on my apologies."

His apologies were duly noted by the wise heads who, to a woman, were disappointed that they would not learn Lord Ranchester's innermost secrets, but never mind, they said, it was understandable really that Mr Gudgeon should feel unable to divulge them. Mrs Davis pointed out that perhaps there was some dark secret, but the village ladies did not rise to that idea.

Mr Gudgeon, meanwhile, continued his daily perambulations around the village, wishing all and sundry a good morning and hurrying on his way. Until the day of the summer fete, that is, when word spread faster than a forest fire that Mr Gudgeon and Mrs Overend were on their way to the event...arm in arm.

"This is such a happy day," Mrs Overend told any fete-goer who would listen on that sunny afternoon. And all the time she kept a limpet-like grip on Mr Gudgeon's arm as he beamed approvingly at her freshly-permed hair and immaculate tailored blue suit.

"I think marriage will suit us very well indeed," he said with a huge smile.

Mrs Overend cooed gently, and said in a voice that fairly bubbled with happiness: "Whoever would have thought that childhood sweethearts would get together again after all these years."

Chapter 3
The Crime Wave

"There was a time when you didn't need to lock anything up. You could leave your front door wide open and know you'd get back and nobody would have been in your house," Mrs Barnes told her fellow WI members at the monthly meeting.

"Not now," said Mrs Ferguson, "you can't so much as turn your back now and it's gone. Terrible state of affairs, if you ask me." Mrs Ferguson told her tut-tutting colleagues: "You can't have anything nice these days before someone comes along and steals it. It's disgusting."

"Come, come, ladies, I do believe that is quite an exaggeration," said Mrs Gladman from the chair. "Little Bardon is hardly The Bronx. But as there has been concern and disquiet in the village of late, I have invited Pc Nicholls along this afternoon to talk to us about crime prevention and perhaps give us a little insight into his role as a police officer."

The affable young policeman talked at length about locks and bolts, about keeping an eye on each other's property and personal safety both at home and outside.

Then he told them: "We are very lucky in Little Bardon, we are in a very low crime area."

"I really have to disagree with you there, constable, there is more crime around here than any of us realise," said Mrs Barnes. "Take last Thursday, one of my elderly neighbours had one of her gnomes stolen. Not the crime of the century, but very worrying, nonetheless."

Pc Nicholls said yes, he knew about the stolen gnome, but suspected it was children playing a prank.

"Children don't leave ransom notes made up from words and letters cut out of newspapers," said Mrs Ferguson. "No, this is something much more serious. We constantly hear about terrorists and the dreadful things they do, and now it's here in the heart of our village, how do we know who is here watching our every move, ready to strike?"

"With respect, we can rule out terrorists. I really can't imagine any terrorist singling out a garden gnome, so please don't worry. Just remember the tips I have given you this afternoon about keeping yourselves and your property safe," said Pc Nicholls, as he left to pursue other less arduous police duties.

"It wasn't just any gnome, it was Charlie, who had been fishing in Miss Green's pond for many happy years. Miss Green said good morning to Charlie every day, and now he is gone. It is heartbreaking," said Mrs Barnes, visibly upset at the thought that Charlie could be in the hands of desperate terrorists.

There were nods of agreement around the room, then Mrs Johnson piped up: "It's not just Charlie who's disappeared. The Burtons in Mill Road have lost Timmy, who has been in their family for many years. One day he was there in the front garden, and the next he was gone. He was such a happy little chap, with his lovely blue and red outfit and big smile."

This was now a worrying development, the ladies agreed, and Mrs Ferguson declared in a loud voice: "It looks like we've got gnomenappers in the village."

"Was there a ransom note?" asked Mrs Barnes. No, there was no ransom note, she was told, just a bare patch of earth where Timmy had stood for years, smiling happily at visitors as they came through Mr and Mrs Burton's front gate.

"Ladies, ladies, ladies, I don't think we should get carried away over this. Pc Nicholls has assured us that these are definitely not acts of terrorism, more likely children and their idea of fun. It is not my idea, of course, and undoubtedly not yours, but fun nonetheless," said Mrs Gladman.

"Now come along ladies, let's move on to the next part of the meeting, chop chop."

But then came the hammer blow. Miss Smith confided that she hadn't liked to say anything, because she didn't want to make a fuss, but she had noticed on her way to the meeting that the memorial seat on the village green had disappeared. Her comment brought gasps from the audience, and one of two of the more nervous among them queried among themselves whether it was going to be safe to walk home alone from the meeting.

Things were getting very serious now, said Mrs Ferguson, who told the ladies: "Two thefts could be a coincidence, but not three. No, this is a targeted attack on this village. We need to be extremely vigilant. One policeman and Neighbourhood Watch are simply not enough."

Mrs Barnes chimed in with doubts about whether Pc Nicholls, while very nice, was really the best man for the job of protecting them from something as serious as this. "It's all very well to tell us we live in a low crime area, and we are perfectly safe, but does he really know? Has he ever dealt with a serious crime wave?"

Wise old heads nodded and there was a general consensus that Little Bardon was a village under siege, if not from terrorists, then perhaps from a dangerous crime syndicate that was preparing some heinous act.

As they walked home in little groups from the meeting there were furtive glances and whispered conversations about whether someone should ring the Chief Constable or perhaps – and this was Mrs Ferguson's suggestion – speak to the editor of the Daily Telegraph to bring it to national attention.

"Or The Sun," said Mrs Barnes. "No, no, definitely not the Sun, let us keep this on a civilised level," retorted Mrs Ferguson.

All of the ladies reached their front doors safely and hurried inside to await news of the next atrocity to hit the village, and there would surely be one, they agreed. It was just a matter of time.

Their eyes and ears would be Iris the postwoman, who cycled the length and breadth of the village every morning, and knew just about everything that was going on, although, as she was quick to point out: "You know me, I'm not one to gossip."

Over the next few days, there was a lot of curtain-twitching and Miss Smith even started noting down the numbers of cars passing through the village, although farmer Reggie Naylor couldn't really fathom why she had written down the number on the back of his big green John Deere tractor.

"You don't need my number," he told her. "You've known me all your life, we went to primary school together." But Miss Smith was adamant – she had been given the task of noting down numbers and she was not going to shirk her duty.

Reggie was still shaking his head in disbelief when he got back to Great Wick Farm. "They've gone barmy in the village, there must be something in the water," he told son Jim.

Back in the village, eyes were watching and ears were twitching as the WI ladies started a surveillance operation co-ordinated by Mrs Ferguson, backed by her able lieutenant Mrs Barnes; Iris the postwoman was their mobile unit spying out the land as she moved through the village, and Miss Smith was desperately trying to get her ballpoint pen to work so she could keep writing down numbers.

They knew it could be a long operation, but this was being nosey with a purpose, although the purpose was lost on some people – by the third day some were feeling a little jaded, and somewhat disappointed that their efforts were not producing sightings of any culprits, and nothing else had been stolen.

By day six most were definitely fed up, and anyone walking through the village would barely see a curtain twitch, although Miss Smith was still diligent in her role as car number recorder, and had filled several pages of her notebook, including two more entries for Reggie Naylor's tractor.

Then something quite unexpected happened. Miss Smith, with notebook at the ready, spotted a truck drive into the village and stop by the green, and was taking its number when she saw something familiar on the back. She waved to the driver and demanded: "Where are you going with that? It's our bench."

Yes, he pointed out, they knew whose bench it was, they were returning it from the council depot after repairing it.

She hurried to report back to Mrs Ferguson, and on the way spotted Charlie back in his familiar spot. It turned out that some youngsters had returned him last night, accompanied by a parent who made them apologise to Miss Green and hand over a box of mint creams as a recompense.

Miss Smith was fairly bursting with these two pieces of good news to relay to Mrs Ferguson, and on the way met Mrs Barnes, who had just found out that Timmy hadn't really been stolen, but had been taken home by the Burtons' son, to superglue his broken arm.

"Wonderful news," said Mrs Ferguson when they reached her door. "We are officially crime-free. It's a marvellous feeling to know we live in a safe, secure community."

Then Iris came puffing and panting along the road. "Iris, where's your bike? It's unusual to see you on your round without it."

Iris gave the three ladies a forlorn look. "Somebody's stolen it."

Chapter 4

The Mysterious Colonel Crawford

Colonel Crawford had only been living at The Grange for a few months when some of Little Bardon's wise old heads started asking questions.

"There's something about him don't ring true," said Norman the vegetable king as he gazed longingly into his empty glass. He looked as if the weight of the world had suddenly been lifted off his shoulders as he came to the momentous decision to have a fill-up.

"Another pint and bag of scratchings, Peggy love," he said with a smile as he shook coins out of his battered leather wallet and on to the polished top of the public bar in the King's Head.

"There's more to that old boy than meets the eye; he's only been here five minutes and thinks he's lord of the blasted manor," said Dennis, whose mere 12 years in the village meant he was still regarded as something of a newcomer himself.

The Colonel - as he insisted on being called by everyone in the village - was something of a mystery man. He had moved to The Grange, a classic, if somewhat careworn, Georgian house on the edge of the village, at the end of summer, after old Mrs Moncrieff passed away unexpectedly.

She had lived there for more than 50 years, nearly 10 of them alone after her husband Gilbert met an unfortunate end when his old Riley car hit a deer on the half-mile drive home from a rather too-convivial evening in the King's Head and poor Gilbert head-butted the windscreen with seemingly considerable force.

"He'd had more than a few whiskies," Miss Smith had confided to all and sundry in the post office at the time.

"She wasn't exactly a stranger to drink, either, was she. I've seen her well the worse for wear. But we mustn't speak ill of the dead, must we." Old heads shook solemnly.

Mrs Moncrieff certainly hadn't been a stranger to drink, particularly a certain brand of sweet sherry, and it had often been said that she spent more with Cray and Walker, the wine merchants in Malbury, than she did on food.

But whatever else they may have been, the Moncrieffs had always taken an active role in village life, Gilbert on the parish council and a stalwart of the King's Head, and Mrs Moncrieff always busy with some activity or other at St Stephen's, where she had been a chorister in her younger days and, after Gilbert's untimely death, an enthusiastic arranger of church flowers.

Haughty Colonel Crawford was hardly a replacement for the affable Mrs Moncrieff in village life, and it was difficult to find anyone who actually liked him - impossible, in fact.

He had got off to the worst possible start on his first day in the village when he told the chattering classes in the post office to get a move on, as he hadn't got all day to stand around listening to idle gossip.

If he had wanted to alienate the village, he couldn't have made a better job of it than to say that to Mrs Gill, Mrs Ferguson and the ever-receptive ear of Miss Smith behind the counter.

"Well, I never, who does he think he is?" said a red-faced Mrs Gill as the tweed-clad but somewhat down-at-heel figure of Colonel

Crawford disappeared out of the door, clutching a book of second class stamps.

"He's the new bloke just moved in to The Grange, he's a general or something, and a very rude one at that," said Miss Smith.

Even before Colonel Crawford arrived back at his new home, the jungle drums were beating fast and furious, with a story of rude behaviour becoming a tale of a fierce verbal altercation and, by the end of the day, of an unholy scene with a catalogue of abuse directed by Colonel Crawford towards the gossips.

It might be said that things could only get better, but they didn't, of course, with the village's newest resident the subject of the majority of conversations whenever two or more locals were within babbling distance of one another.

Colonel Crawford was seldom seen in the village, and then usually only driving through behind the wheel of his old Bentley, a car which had definitely seen better days; in fact, some said, a bit like him.

A Mrs Crawford was rumoured to be in residence, but was never seen, although a woman with expensive-looking suitcase was spotted one Friday evening arriving in a taxi from Malbury station, and, as Mrs Davis was keen to impart to whoever would listen, she was definitely 'tarty'.

That nugget of information was enough to get the rumour mill running at double speed, especially as Mrs Davis insisted the woman had never left.

As the months passed, The Grange and the activities of its occupants largely disappeared from the daily gossiping agenda. There were the odd attempted forays into Colonel Crawford's background, but none could decipher the clues to his past.

Until, that is, Joe the plasterer told his darts team mates in the King's Head one night: "That old colonel ain't." "Ain't what?" asked Norman, as he chalked a treble twenty. "Ain't a colonel, he used to be a milkman somewhere up in Suffolk."

"How do you know that?" asked Norman. "He could have been a milkman AND a colonel."

"My mate Don from Halesworth came down on Sunday to bring me some fancy bantams and old Crawford drove past in that old car of his. 'Blow me,' said Don, 'I don't believe it, that's old Jimmy Crawford. I wondered what happened to him after he got the push from the milk round for working a fiddle. Some said he didn't need to do it because he'd been left a lot of money.'"

Word of this revelation flew around the village at lightning speed; by the morning, it was the main topic of conversation everywhere that wise heads met.

"What did I tell you," exclaimed an excited Mrs Davis. "I knew he was a wrong'un, and now we all know, don't we. Colonel Goldtop, more like."

And so the name stuck.

A week or two later, Norman was standing idly in his large garden, leaning on a digging fork and admiring his bantams - those pretty little miniature chickens whose eggs he sold at the gate by the half dozen - when a big car raced past at speed.

Blimey, he thought, that old Crawford is in a hurry. The next car past his gate was in even more of a hurry, blue lights flashing and siren screaming.

It was the most excitement Norman had had for years, and he wasn't going to miss out on this opportunity to be the centre of attention when he relayed the events later in the public bar at the King's Head.

He wheeled his trusty old bicycle out from its home in the coal shed, and pedalled furiously - furiously for Norman, that is, but a bit like competing in a schooldays slow bicycle race for anyone else - in the direction of The Grange, a quarter of a mile away

He arrived just in time to see the police car drive out of the gate and off in the direction of Malbury, with Colonel Goldtop in the back seat.

At that moment, the village went into meltdown; Norman was so excited and so desperate to spread the news that he fell off his bicycle into a patch of stinging nettles, but not before he shouted: "Old Goldtop's just bin nicked," to Mrs Ferguson waiting for the Malbury bus at the stop just along the road.

In fact, it was trying to do two things at once - cycle and shout - that upset his equilibrium and put him into an irretrievable wobble. "First time I've fell off that old bike since the night we had that yard of ale contest," he told them later in the King's Head.

"Don't talk to me about that night," said Joe. "I fell upstairs when I got home and she made me sleep with the dog. But don't worry about that now, what about old Goldtop. Does anyone know what's been going on?"

No-one knew, of course, but there was wild speculation that Colonel Goldtop might be a murderer, bank robber or even a gun runner. Someone even suggested that it might have been him who had stolen Iris the postwoman's bike the week before.

"I don't think they'd have sent a police car for a nicked bike," said Joe knowingly as he took aim at the treble nineteen.

The speculation continued until Peggy called Last Orders and Norman, Joe and the rest of the regulars staggered out into the night, and it continued through the week.

Until Thursday, when the *Malbury and District Recorder* popped through letter boxes. Miss Smith was quick to the phone: "Have you seen the paper?" she spluttered excitedly to Mrs Davis. "Old Goldtop's a hero. That police car wasn't because he was being arrested, it was to take him to hospital because he's got a rare blood group and they needed the blood for someone who had been in a bad accident. 'Colonel James saves the day', the headline says."

"He's a rum 'un, old Goldtop, and no mistake," Dennis muttered into his third pint in the King's Head that evening, and sage heads the length of the bar nodded in agreement.

I'M NOT ONE TO GOSSIP

The Crawford saga was soon regarded as yesterday's news, and the village moved on to a new topic of conversation....until the *Malbury and District Recorder* appeared three weeks later with a letter from someone called Tompkins saying that Crawford had served in his regiment, and had never risen above the rank of Lance Corporal.

The *Recorder* said it had tried to secure an interview with the seemingly bogus colonel, but he had not responded to any of the messages left.

It did, however, report that an anonymous villager had revealed that Crawford was widely known as Colonel Goldtop.

Crawford wasn't seen again. His occasional forays into the village stopped, and there was no sign of life at The Grange, which was a disappointment to the gossiping fraternity who had hoped to benefit from Norman's twice-daily excursions past there on his bike.

Then one day, Norman ran - albeit at a somewhat leisurely pace - into the post office and shared with the pension queue that a For Sale sign was being erected outside The Grange at that very moment.

"Well, I'll be blowed, no more Goldtop," said Mrs Gill, as the queue pondered on what the next item of gossip might be.

"That reminds me," said Mrs Gladman, "that new milkman seems to spend a lot of time round one of those new houses in Mill Road."

And so the village returned to normal, with gossiping equilibrium restored.

Chapter 5

Miss Meacham's Cat

The old lady in black seemed to live a singularly solitary life, in a private world hidden behind firmly drawn curtains and a ferocious scowl.

In the short time they had been neighbours he had only actually seen her a handful of times, and on each occasion she looked even more fearsome than the time before.

When he moved in, he had assumed the cottage next door was empty; it looked completely run down, and the garden was a jungle. Then a few evenings later he had a fleeting glimpse of the old lady in the garden, but by the time he had gone outside to talk to her, she had gone.

He first bumped into her - almost literally – a month or so after moving in to his little weekend cottage, when he was woken in the early hours of a bitterly cold November morning by a constant tapping that he thought at first was the metallic clanking of rigging against the masts of the yachts sitting indolently on their moorings on the nearby river.

But no, as he lay listening in the eerie stillness, he could tell that this was a different noise, a persistent tap, tap, tap, that, once he was a little more awake, sounded more like something tapping on glass - a tree on a window pane, perhaps?

Now he was fully awake, and thought he ought to have a quick look outside, in case a branch had fallen against the cottage. As he opened the back door and took in the fresh marshland air, he was aware of movement in the garden next door, and from somewhere in the night came the sound of a muffled voice.

As he yawningly wondered who on earth could be outside at 3am, the old lady's straggly head emerged suddenly from the gloom, looking as startled at his appearance as he was at hers.

"Is everything okay?" he called over the fence. "Looking for my cat," she replied gruffly as she hurried back into the darkness.

You live and learn, he thought, as he slid gratefully back into his still-warm bed. He had lived next door to her for several weeks - albeit only at weekends - and didn't even know she had a cat. Come to think of it, he didn't even know her name.

He didn't see her again for a month or so. Of course, there was no reason he should have seen his only neighbour very often, because he usually arrived late on Friday evening and left early on Monday morning. Although, when he thought about it now, surely he should have expected to see something of her at weekends, even if only pottering in that overgrown garden?

It was a cold and foggy early January evening when he next saw her; she was hovering around her back door, as if waiting for someone. Maybe the cat that he had still not seen had gone missing again.

"Good evening, happy new year," he called to her disappearing back as she slid silently back towards the doorway, without so much as a nod of recognition.

He had tried to drop the obligatory neighbourly Christmas card through her letter box the weekend before, but found the box sealed as tight as her curtains. This is one very strange old lady, he thought, as he mused on the fact that her cottage was always dark and silent.

It was almost as if no-one actually lived there.

In fact, unless you knew that it was inhabited, you would be forgiven for thinking that the tiny weatherboarded building was empty. Because of its semi-derelict condition and neglected garden, when he had first viewed his own cottage he had assumed the neighbouring one was as unlived in as it appeared unloved.

His own cottage was a bolthole from the City, a refuge not only from a busy weekday life but also from a messy divorce. It was his place of solitude and contentment, his place to get his head together again; and he didn't want to share it with anyone - just yet.

But his bucolic weekend idyll was not all it seemed; soon after Christmas, life in the cottage started to change.

First there was the succession of dead birds on his doorstep when he got up in the morning. But he put that down to his neighbour's mysterious cat. As theirs were the only two cottages in the lane down to the seawall, it seemed a logical conclusion.

Then he started waking in the night to strange noises that seemed to come from deep within the walls of the cottage. Oh well, he told himself, old wooden-framed buildings do move a bit.

But despite sometimes feeling melancholy and very alone when he was in the cottage, he generally enjoyed being there.....until a Saturday night in early February when his life was turned upside down.

He had stayed in London on the Friday night to go out with friends, and only arrived at the cottage on a bitterly cold Saturday afternoon.

By the time he had a fire roaring in the grate it was dark and forbidding outside and the malt whisky bottle was inviting, so he did nothing to resist as the evening disappeared in a haze of alcohol-fuelled memories; he pulled a blanket over himself on the sofa and settled into a fitful sleep.

He didn't know how long he had been asleep when he woke with a start and stared into the room's inky blackness, a dreadful panic coming over him as he tried to reason with the unmistakeable feeling of not being alone. The very walls seemed to be talking to him and he could feel the hairs on his neck standing up like bristles as his eyes fought to see through the blackness and his head fought against the pounding the whisky had left behind.

As his head cleared and his eyes became accustomed to the darkness, he had a terrible feeling that he was staring directly into the eyes of an animal - a cat, sitting on the table just a few feet away. And it was staring back at him so intensely and so malevolently, that he had to look away; he simply could not bear to look at it.

He opened his eyes again, and it was gone, and a huge feeling of relief came over him, and he knew it must simply be his whisky-fuelled imagination working overtime.

But then he felt warm breath against his cheek, and as he turned his head slightly he saw the horrible creature just inches from his face, staring with dreadful eyes that bored through his head, and he had an overpowering feeling that it did not want him there.

His throat was dry, his head was pounding, and he was more terrified than he had ever believed he could be.

He held his breath and felt he wanted to cry out, but no sound came, and then the monstrous cat - be it real or imagined - was gone again. He lay still for what seemed an eternity, then, as he slowly turned his head, he sensed that the animal was somewhere in the dark shadows in the corner of the room.

And then the most terrible thing happened - as he looked into the face of the cat he saw it start to change; its features twisted into a hideous grimace that shifted and contorted until now it was the old lady, and he could see her as clearly as in daylight.

In a blink the cat was back, staring straight into his eyes as if it were trying to tell him something. It moved closer, so close that he could hear its purring, and it still kept coming closer and he was sure now that it was willing him to go.

Then he heard the old lady's gruff voice telling him the same thing, and he was frozen in fear so intense that he could do no more than shut his eyes tight and pray for this hideous dream to end. He wanted to open them, to try to end this nightmare, but could not.

Just as panic started to overwhelm him, he sensed a movement and felt something brushing against his cheek. Then he heard the old lady's voice, but now it seemed to be coming not from in the room, but from outside.

She was calling the cat.

Was he dreaming, or was this real? It couldn't be real, could it? It must be the whisky, or just a horrible dream. He lay there the rest of the night, not knowing whether he was really awake, or in the middle of an indescribable nightmare.

He lay petrified, with the blanket pulled tight around him; as dawn threw its light through the thin curtains, he found the courage to get up and look around the tiny front room. The front door was locked and bolted, the window was securely fastened and the room's other door, leading to the kitchen, was closed - and there was no cat.

Then as he passed the mirror over the mantelpiece, in the nearly-light of morning he saw a face that he did not want to own, a pallid, wretched face with dark-ringed eyes and - oh my God, he thought - a scratch across the cheek.

He knew then what he must do if he were to retain his sanity; he packed a bag straight away, locked up and hurried, half stumbling, out to his car to get as far away as possible.

As he closed the boot he thought he could hear a chuckle from the next door garden, but he darted a glance across the fence and there was no-one there.

Next morning, from the sanctuary of his City office, he phoned the agent who rented him the cottage, and told him he was moving out.

"You lasted longer than I expected," the man said. "You're the umpteenth tenant in that cottage. The solitude of being the only house for nearly a mile seems to get to everyone in the end."

"The only house? What about the one next door?" the man asked him.

"That hasn't been lived in for 30 years, ever since old Miss Meacham died," said the agent. "Apparently the man living in your cottage poisoned her cat and the old girl died, they say, of a broken heart.

"Sad really, because all she ever wanted was to spend the rest of her life with that cat."

Chapter 6

Walter Woolacombe's Big Trip

Walter Woolacombe loved what he called his 'little trips'. With his brother Harold he was known to venture almost as far as the county boundary to enjoy the excitement of traction engine rallies, heavy horse shows and country fairs.

He once even contemplated an excursion over the boundary to Ipswich to visit the Suffolk Show, but Harold said he wouldn't drive that far, and if Walter wanted to go he would have to find someone else to take him, or else get the bus.

"There ain't a bus all the way from Little Bardon to Ipswich. I'd have to change two or three times and that would take all day," said Walter.

The plan was quietly dropped, and the brothers contented themselves with planning little trips of a more local nature - trips rather more in keeping with the capabilities of a man of Harold's advanced age, and of a car that looked almost as old as Harold.

Walter's little trips were adventures that he talked about to anyone who would listen.

"Did I tell you about Sunday?" Walter asked Peggy, the barmaid in the King's Head. "That was a lovely little trip to the vintage tractor show, they had one of them old Fordson tractors that Harold used to drive."

"Yes, you've told me about that," said Peggy, stifling a yawn.

"What a day we had, me and Harold, but he called me a rum old fool when I bought one of them old candy flosses. I'll have another pint, Peggy love."

"When's your next trip then, Walter?" asked Norman, who used to work on the Co-op coal lorry, but now spent most of his retirement on his allotment, where he grew the most amazing vegetables.

Not surprisingly, Norman would share with no-one the secrets of growing the finest vegetables in the area; in fact, the finest vegetables in the county, according to some.

"I haven't been feeling so good lately Norman, so I ain't really sure when my next little trip will be. I might have to give up travelling about so much until the weather gets a bit warmer. Perhaps I'll spend a bit more time on my vegetables instead. See if I can take the cup off you at next year's show, eh."

"That'll be about right," said Norman with a chuckle.

Walter was joking about winning the cup, of course, because Norman had won it at the village show every year since time immemorial, but the very fact that Walter was talking about giving up travelling - albeit temporarily - was worrying to those around him who overheard.

"I never thought I'd hear old Walter have a conversation without a mention of where he was off to next," said Peggy to Joe the plasterer, standing a little farther along the bar. "He must be ill."

As Walter walked the short distance home, he reflected on some of those wonderful little trips he had enjoyed over the years: ploughing matches, flower shows, heavy horse shows.

It was heavy horses that were going to figure in the special trip that he had been thinking about for a while. He had always loved watching them work on the farms when he was a young man, and enjoyed seeing them even more now when they paraded in front of him and Harold in the show ring.

He loved the way they moved, the way the brasses on their harness glistened in the sunlight and the way their beautifully plaited manes and tails finished off this picture of rural charm.

Walter could imagine how it would be to arrive in the village riding on a farm waggon behind a pair of plodding Shires.

"That's what I want to do," he told Harold when he got home. "I want to ride into the village in style. That's the way I'd like to travel, and blow me if that ain't something I'm going to arrange."

Harold shook his head: "I don't think there's a lot of chance of that, Walter. Reggie Naylor's still got a pair of Shires and a Norfolk waggon, but I don't think he'd do that for the likes of you and me."

Pneumonia laid Walter low that winter and planning trips was the last thing on his mind, but Harold started laying plans so that his dearly-loved brother was not disappointed.

The day of the trip came, and this was one that Walter would be taking alone: the big trip he had said he had dreamed of taking, but only when he was good and ready.

"I want to ride into the village on Reggie's waggon, behind Major and Tommy, and I want their harness to shine and their coats to gleam, so everyone looks and says what a lucky old beggar Walter is to travel like that," he had told Harold.

Harold and Reggie planned the trip between them; Harold wanted to make Walter's dream come true, and Reggie loved any opportunity to harness up Major and Tommy and show off his beloved horses.

Harold spent hours washing and polishing the blue and red paintwork on Reggie's farm waggon, while Reggie and his son spent as many hours braiding and plaiting manes and tails to make Major and Tommy look the magnificent animals that they were.

Walter was on a platform on the back of the waggon for the three mile trip through the lanes that he loved so much to the village that had been his home for so many years.

The sight of the trundling waggon pulled by the beautifully turned-out horses stopped the little local traffic that there was that day, and brought people out of their houses to have a look.

Reggie sat proudly behind his horses, which never put a foot wrong as they plodded up the hill and into the village, and he had even smartened himself up for the occasion. He had agreed with Harold that this should be a very special trip for Walter, and had done everything he could to ensure that it was something that the whole village would remember.

When they arrived at their destination in the village, Reggie turned and said: "Here we are, Walter old mate. I'd like to think you've enjoyed the trip," then turned back to his horses and blew hard into a big red handkerchief.

Walter's big trip - the one he had been so determined to make and the one that Harold was equally determined he would - ended a few minutes later with his friends around him and the words of the Reverend Nigel Stollery ringing in everyone's ears: "We commit the body of our dear brother Walter...."

Chapter 7

The Marrow

"Hey, Norman, seen this?" said Young Fred as he burst through the door of the King's Head, dripping with January rain and holding aloft a page torn out of a gardening magazine. "Some old boy in Wales has grown a marrow three times bigger than your show-winner last year."

"Rubbish," said a disgruntled Norman, putting his pint glass down on the bar. "They print any old rubbish in the papers. That's why I never buy one."

"Sure that's not because you can't read?" Dennis threw in to the fledgeling conversation. "Of course I can read, I did the football pools for years," said Norman. "A-hah, but you never won the treble chance, did you," retorted Dennis.

There were puzzled looks along the bar as the gathered company mused over any possible connection between winning the treble chance and an ability to read. Then, to a man, they went back to their pints and pork scratchings.

"Anyway, this is *Garden News* and not a paper, so it's going to be true. This old boy has grown a record-breaking marrow that weighs 255 pounds and is over five feet long. And if you don't believe it you can read it for yourself," said Young Fred. "Blimey, that's nearly twice as heavy as me. How does it fare against you, Peggy love?"

"Mind your own business, you cheeky young sod," said Peggy from behind the bar. Peggy could fairly be described as buxom, a stereotype of the jolly barmaid, and had an intimate acquaintance with an encyclopaedia of diets; the current one featured copious amounts of pomegranate seeds washed down with a drop of gin. Of course. it had never been established whether her nightly consumption of gin and tonic actually aided any of her diets, as she claimed, but she said it made losing weight more pleasurable.

"Mine were 82 pound, and that were good enough to win the red rosette, which now hangs over my mantelpiece," said Norman, with a glint in his eye. "Yes, but this old boy's in the paper is 255 pounds, and you'll never beat that," said Young Fred.

"I'll show you whether I can beat it or not. It just takes a bit of planning, and plenty of knowledge. If any of you old boys fancy having a go, let's make it interesting and have a little bet."

And so the great marrow growing contest began, and what better man to throw down the gauntlet than Norman, Little Bardon's undisputed vegetable king. "I'll take on all comers," he said with a confident smile, and a raise of his pint glass.

"Count me in," said Dennis, with the familiar barking cough that came from smoking too many of the cheap smuggled cigarettes that his nephew Jack sold slyly at the Sunday car boot sale in Malbury. "I've grown some big old courgettes, so I reckon I can manage a decent sized marrow."

"And me," said Fred senior, whose previous vegetable growing expertise had been limited to a couple of rows of potatoes every year, and a row or two of peas. "I'll help you, dad," said Young Fred. "I reckon we've got the makings of a winning team. Two more pints over here, Peggy love."

The consensus of opinion along the length of the public bar that night was that the three entries should be grown from the same batch of seed, and that the best time to plant them was mid-April. Beyond that, it was every man for himself, at least it was once it had been agreed that the two losers should each buy the winner a gallon of beer after a weigh-in in the pub at Michaelmas, September 29.

The seed was eventually bought, after much discussion over copious amounts of beer, and two seeds allocated to each contestant.

Norman recruited Joe as his wingman, Dennis teamed up with Sid, and Young Fred joined Fred senior in the great marrow growing challenge. The gauntlet had been thrown down, picked up and properly christened with a few pints of Old Todger.

Over the next few weeks, furtive conversations between team members became a public bar commonplace, as wise heads decided their various marrow-growing strategies, with Peggy hovering discreetly in the background, but with an ear always receptive to conversations.

With no time to waste, the three teams started their preparations in earnest, and in secret, with brothers Joe and Sid particularly furtive with one another. Village vegetable king Norman was clear favourite to win, so Sid did everything he could to entice brother Joe to spill a secret of Norman's or two, but even a bellyful of Old Todger wasn't enough to loosen his lips.

Pits were dug, barrowloads of well-rotted cow manure shoveled in, and the great marrow contest was under way, with each team ready to plant its two seeds.

"How's it going?" Peggy asked Fred senior one evening as she pushed another pint of Old Todger across the bar. "Don't say anything, Peggy love, but I think we're going to win this," said Fred senior. "We've got a nice bit of horticultural sand spread over the cow muck."

Peggy gave a nod and moved along the bar and asked Dennis the same question. "We've got our seed growing under some gentle heat, and did you know you have to plant the seed on edge to prevent rotting, then when we plant out we'll feed with tomato food for a couple of weeks," said Dennis. "I know you won't say anything, Peggy love, so I don't mind telling you.'

And so it went through the summer, with conversations whispered over pints of Old Todger, and Peggy used as a sort of silent sounding board for marrow-growing best practice; each of the secrets was received with a knowing smile and a nod.

She heard across the bar about watering and feeding regimes, about Gordon the gardener being called in to pollinate the plants and about Norman's most secret of secrets concerning his reason for blagging some stale beer to take home. "I'll have a drop of that ullage, save throwing it away," he told Peggy with a wink.

By early August, growing marrows became a nightly topic of public bar conversation, with lots of nods and winks and good-natured banter about who was going to take the coveted prize of a gallon of beer from each of the two losing teams.

Then came disaster. "One of mine has split," a devastated Fred senior confided in Peggy one evening. "I think I must have over-watered." And with that he slunk off into a corner of the bar, waiting to break the news to Young Fred when he came in for his usual after-work pint.

"Dad, dad, you'll never guess what's happened," shouted an excited Young Fred as he charged through the door. "I know what's happened," said a despondent Fred senior, "but why are you so happy about it?"

"I thought you'd be happy as well, it gives us a better chance." A puzzled Fred senior asked: "A better chance of what?" "Of winning the competition, of course," replied Young Fred.

"How can us losing one of our marrows help us?" said Fred senior. "What? No, I was going to tell you about one of Mrs Gill's goats getting in to Dennis' garden and making a heck of a mess, including destroying one of his marrows." It was the first time Fred senior had smiled since arriving at the pub.

As August gave way to September, the atmosphere in the public bar became increasingly fraught and furtive, as the three teams and their various supporters whispered in corners and continued to consume Old Todger in industrial quantities. "You didn't hear none of that, did you Peggy love," was heard regularly, and met with "Hear any of what?"

A week before the weigh-in, landlord Charlie announced that he was borrowing a set of heavy-duty scales from Sampsons, the animal feed suppliers in Malbury, and that Pc Nicholls would be the official scrutineer.

The village turned out in force for the big event, putting a huge smile on Charlie's face as the till worked overtime.

The three teams wheeled in their entries, hidden under old sacking and – in Dennis' case – what was rumoured to be his wife's dressing gown.

"Are we all ready then?" asked Pc Nicholls, who was always happy to be part of village activities when he was off-duty. "Let's just have another pint or two first," said Dennis, as he drained his Old Todger and pushed the glass across to Peggy for a refill.

The moment came, coins were tossed to decide the weighing order, and a beaming Fred senior unveiled a handsome-looking marrow that brought a few gasps from the increasingly inebriated crowd in the bar.

"Ninety eight pounds and four ounces," said Pc Nicholls. When the clapping stopped, Dennis produced his best effort. "Ninety four pounds dead," Pc Nicholls told the disappointed grower, who stood aside to let Norman wheel his giant effort to the scales.

"One hundred and thirty pounds and eight ounces," declared Pc Nicholls. "I declare Norman and Joe the winners."

But then Peggy called out: "Just hang on a minute. I'm not in the contest, but I would like all you marrow-growing experts to have a look at something," and with Charlie's assistance heaved a huge marrow on to the scales.

"One hundred and thirty two pounds and two ounces," said Pc Nicholls, to ecstatic clapping and cheers.

"Who grew that?" asked an incredulous Norman. "Not you, Peggy love, it can't have been." "You daft sods have been confiding in me for months, with your fancy ideas for growing the biggest marrow, so I thought I would have a go myself."

With that the pub erupted into laughter and shouts of "Well done, Peggy love" and "Good for you, Peggy, you've shown 'em how to do it."

"Fair dues to you, Peggy love," said Norman. "I think you've earned a few gins tonight, because you've certainly taught us to keep our big mouths shut."

Chapter 8

Old Morton

You didn't look twice at Old Morton. You wanted to, but you knew that if you did you would meet the stare of those cold, dark eyes that hid a thousand secrets.

Eyes that you were sure saw everything you did and knew every move you made. Eyes that you knew had seen things in other places that must never be spoken about. Dreadful, gimlet-like eyes that made the hairs on the back of your neck stand on end.

Old Morton lived a mile or so outside Little Bardon in a ramshackle cottage at the end of a rutted farm track on a flat Essex peninsula that lies between two rivers. A cottage where the curtains were always closed and a welcome was never extended.

His weatherboarded home with its long-peeled paint and rickety fence was the last outpost between the warm hearths of the village and the cold waters of the North Sea. It was in the middle of that no man's land of reclaimed marsh sitting inside the sea wall which has now been bulldozed into huge fields to grow cereal crops.

It was said that no visitor had been inside it in the 30 or more years since Old Morton's sister went away, and no-one could actually remember anyone being welcomed inside before that.

He and his sister had lived together in that tiny cottage, where their parents before them had lived a hard life and died unknown and unloved by the community whose boundaries they seldom crossed, either physically or spiritually.

Old Morton had followed his father on to the farm where he worked the horses and learned the hard way that a man has to walk eleven miles to plough an acre in a day with a pair of Shires.

But he was happy with his lot, and he wasn't Old Morton then. The farm foreman called him Jim and his sister called him James, and in the village he was Mr Morton when he cycled in once every few weeks to buy groceries.

But even then, no-one in the village ever really knew him, or his sister. In fact, no-one could really remember seeing his sister more than once or twice after she left the village school.

"She allus kept herself to herself," Mrs Barnes at the bakery would say. "I saw her once, when him and her was walkin' down Grange Road, but she never said nothin'. We was at school together, though she was two years younger than me, and was hardly ever there. Pretty girl, she were, so pretty they made her May Queen just before she left. I remember her with her crown of flowers. That were the only time I ever saw her laugh."

Mrs Barnes knew everything about everyone in the village, but she knew next to nothing about Old Morton's family. His father had worked at Grange Farm for years, but was seldom seen in the village, and anyway didn't mix, and his son was the same.

The gaunt frame of Old Morton, in the long brown string-belted overcoat and battered felt trilby he always wore, could sometimes be seen chopping wood for his fire, pottering around his vegetable patch or feeding his few chickens - but to see him meant creeping along the deep fleet ditch bordering his cottage and peering over the top like commandoes on a raid.

To the village boys that was just what they were, bravely stalking Old Morton as he went silently about his chores. Until the day he spotted them and their bravery evaporated.

He never said a word, but then he didn't need to. He just looked at them with those dark eyes that said everything they needed to be told. They said run as fast as you can, get your bikes from the end of the lane and go home. And don't come back.

And they didn't go back, leaving Old Morton to the peace of marshland, to the sounds of widgeon and teal coming in from the sea, the call of the whooper swans swooping in low on bitterly cold and snowy January nights and the chorus of the brent geese feeding on the autumn stubble after their long flight from Siberia.

The years rolled by, and Old Morton was seen even less often in the village. His old bike had rusted away years ago, but he occasionally trudged the mile to the village shop, a treasure trove which housed the post office where he collected his pension. Then the now-stooping figure trudged home again, a can of paraffin in one hand and bag of groceries in the other. And all the time he never spoke a word more than he had to.

The only time a spark was ever seen in those dark eyes was when he stopped to pick a flower from the roadside verge or some may blossom from the hedgerow. For a man whose whole being was dark and foreboding, it always seemed strange that he could stop and pick the most delicate flowers, and walk home holding them as gently as a lover's hand.

And then the rumours started. "There's somethin' funny going on down there," Mrs Barnes, now long retired from the bakery, confided to anyone who would listen. "Them two blokes last week who was taking bird pictures said he shouted at them and shook his fist when they started taking pictures near his cottage. That ain't normal, is it."

From that point Mrs Barnes took an extra interest in Old Morton, but no-one else seemed to care very much about him or what mysteries his cottage might hold. But then, no-one had ever cared much about Old Morton.

The first person to care for a very long time was probably Miss Smith at the post office. "Old Mr Morton hasn't been in to collect his pension for nearly two months, and he hasn't been in the shop for groceries," she told Ben the relief postman one bright May morning.

"I haven't seen him for ages, but I hardly ever do, really, because I always drop what little post he has in his box at the end of the lane," said Ben, who knew almost as much as Mrs Barnes about what happened in the village. "I'll mention it to the policeman if I see him."

The last time the new village policeman was at Old Morton's cottage he was ten years old, and playing commandoes in that fleet ditch. Now, nearly 20 years on, he was going back, and this time he wouldn't let those dark eyes frighten him away.

"It's Pc Nicholls, Mr Morton," he said as he knocked on the bare wooden door. There was no reply, and no audible stirring from inside. He knocked again and again, but the cottage was silent.

"Mr Morton, are you in there? I need to talk to you," he shouted at the door, before walking to the front window where rotting cloth that had once been curtains hung in tatters. Through the holes he stared into black space, where only slivers of light penetrated.

He could make out two wooden armchairs facing an open fireplace and, just as he feared, he could see what he took to be the top of Old Morton's lifeless head.

It didn't take much to force the front door, and as he stood in a pool of light thrown through the open doorway, what he saw took his breath away.

Old Morton was sitting upright in his chair, his face contorted in a smile and his eyes no longer dark and menacing, but soft and gentle as if he had died a truly happy man.

His right hand was stretched across to the chair beside his, delicately holding the skeletal hand of what could only be assumed from the tattered white dress had once been a young woman.

Parchment-like skin was stretched across her cheek bones....and on her head was a crown of wilted wild flowers.

Chapter 9

The Sadness of Miss Day

Jane Day had never married, although, in her younger days she had been a pretty, bubbly girl, always full of life. She had rebuffed potential suitors and had always led a single, simple life – at least, that is how it had always appeared.

She had devoted her life to the generations of children who learned their life lessons at Malbury St Michael's Primary School, and for 30 or more years had been Brown Owl to Little Bardon Brownies.

She was an integral part of the fabric of both town and village, always ready to organise an event, rattle a charity collecting tin or bake cakes for any event that needed them. To everyone she was simply Miss Day, a good sort, although occasionally with a slightly annoying 'jolly hockey sticks' air.

But behind that smiling front there was a darkness that she kept hidden behind a cloak of supreme respectability, a secret that she would share with no-one.

She had been just 22 when she fell in love, and it was a love that was to endure through her life, a love so deep and passionate that it sustained her through even the bleakest of times, when she desperately yearned for him to hold her once more in those powerful arms, arms that had held her on the dancefloor at the Ritz on those wonderful nights they had spent together in London.

But that was a long, long time ago, and life had been very different in those days, when her parents were ecstatically happy that their only daughter was doing so well at teacher training college. They had no idea that Roger Martin had seduced the eager young woman who wanted to cast off the shackles of a strict home and that she was totally besotted with him, and with the secret love they shared.

He was married, but that didn't matter to her, because he had told her that his marriage had been a mistake, and meant nothing to him, and that one day they would be together and would build a wonderful, idyllic life; but first he had to go to Australia for six months to help establish a new office for his family's import-export business.

They had one last, lingering night of passion before he sailed away on that grey and gloomy morning in 1976; Jane hid her sadness behind the mask she was to wear for the rest of her life, a mask of sweetness and eagerness to please.

She marked the days off her calendar, and as those days turned to weeks, and weeks to months, she became more and more desperate to be with her first true love, but achingly sad that she would have to turn her back on the life she had known, leaving behind the parents who would neither understand nor tolerate her love for a married man.

She declared her love every week in the letters she spent hours writing, reading and re-reading before posting, letters that declared her unerring love and helped her get through the week ahead without Roger.

He wrote back to her once a month, in letters she treasured and read over and over – letters that talked about them sharing a new life in Australia, a secret life away from the village.

Then, as spring turned to summer, came the letter she had so desperately awaited. She read if over and over again, with tears of joy coursing down her cheeks:

"Darling Jane, I am truly desperate to be with you. It has been such a long time, but my divorce will soon be finalised, and I cannot wait to make you my wife.

"My ship docks on the 23rd of next month; I will have some paperwork to complete, which will take but a few hours, then I will get the train to London and be with you on the 25th. We will return to Australia and have such a wonderful life together.

"All my love, and much more, your own Roger."

She lay awake all that night, excited at the thought of seeing Roger again, but going over and over in her mind how she would tell her parents, the parents who had given her so much. She cried tears of both joy and sorrow, tears that stained her cheeks with the red marks of love for the three people who meant so much to her.

She marked off the days, one by one, as the 25th grew closer, but still she could not find a way to tell her parents without hurting them grievously.

The morning of the 25th came and went, the afternoon slipped by, and the evening disappeared in a flood of tears, but no Roger. The 26th passed with a terrible feeling that something must have happened to him, but she had no way of contacting him, and didn't even know where he had lived in London, except it was somewhere in Camden.

The shipping company said they could not give her any information, and the telegram she sent to his address in Adelaide did not produce a response.

Where was he? It was a question she asked herself every day as she gradually got back to her life, eventually moving back to live with her parents in Little Bardon, and starting her first teaching job in Malbury.

She became jolly Miss Day, beloved by every child and liked and respected by every adult. She was quite simply the perfect teacher, and friend to all, sharing every part of her life, except her all-consuming love for Roger, whose memory remained locked away for ever.

Then came retirement after a lifetime of unstinting service to the community, and a new chapter started to unfold. Her parents had long passed, but she still lived in the family home in the village, with Bertie and Mabel, her cats, and threw herself into village life.

Outwardly, Jane Day was a happy, contented soul who enjoyed both female and male company, but noticeably never let any man get close to her. What remained shut away was her sadness at the events of so many years ago.

And so the years ticked by until the morning that brought the letter that was to change her life for ever.

"My darling," it began, "it has been so long since we were together, enjoying such wonderful times. So much has happened in that half a lifetime, and I cannot begin to tell you how desperately sorry I am that you were treated so badly.

"The day before I boarded the ship to come back to England I received a letter from my wife informing me that if I persisted in pushing for a divorce, she would take my children out of the country and I would never see them again. I had never told you about my two children because I thought you would no longer want me.

"I am now approaching the end of my life, and would dearly like to hold your hand once more as I tell you I have always loved you, and how desperately sorry I am for the way I have treated you. Your loving Roger."

She sat, stunned, her head swirling, as she let the tears course down her cheeks, tears of joy and tears of fear. What should she do now? He was nearly 50 years in the past, but had never been in the past, he had always been in the present, in her thoughts every day and In her heart every second.

She kept staring at the telephone number on the bottom of the letter, not knowing what to do. She wanted to ring it and hear Roger's voice again, but what would she say? She kept asking herself, over and over again, if that was what she really wanted? He had dumped her all those years ago, and left her with a heart still broken and in pieces.

Did she want to rekindle something that should have died years ago, but never did?

She lay awake most of that night, going over and over in her mind what she should do. She had once been young and pretty, and the sort of young woman any man would be proud to have on his arm, and in his bed, but she had given herself to Roger, given her whole life to Roger, and he had walked away.

Now he wanted her again, but did she want him? Yes, she knew she did, she wanted him desperately.

Jane Day's heart pumped as she dialled the number, and she felt the tiny beads of perspiration on her forehead as she listened to the ring tone. A woman's voice answered, a woman who had obviously been crying.

She asked if she could speak to Roger, and the woman said she was Mary, his daughter. "Is that Jane?" she asked. "He was hoping you would call. I posted the letter for him. It took him an age to write it, because he simply couldn't get the words down on paper."

"Can I speak to him, please? It's been so long, and I have so much I want to say. We were friends a long, long time ago."

"I know, he told me what you meant to him, and he told me he wanted to make amends before it was too late. He loved you until the end."

"The end?"

"He had a really aggressive cancer, and sadly passed away in the hospice this morning. His last words were: 'Tell Jane I am very, very sorry, and that I have always loved her.'"

Chapter 10

Nozzer

"Hello, Nozzer boy, haven't seen you for a while."

"No, Sid, I've been down the treacle mine again.'

"How long you been away this time?"

"Eighteen weeks."

"Same sort of thing as before?"

"Yes, trouble is, you can't ask a man to give up driving, whatever the old judges say. And if they say I shouldn't drive my old car, I can't see why they expect me to have tax and insurance."

"I think the courts do have a bit of a point though, Nozzer, and the trouble is you always seem to get caught," said Sid. "How long do they say you should stay off the road for, this time?"

"Two years," said cheery Nozzer, who lived near Malbury, but was a regular visitor to Little Bardon to see his mother, Norah, who still lived in the cottage where he had been born more than 50 years ago.

He had always been Nozzer, and few people knew that his arch-royalist mum had actually seen fit to name him Charles, and still called him that. Still, he thought, if that makes her happy.

He also tried to make her happy by telling her he was going away to work in the treacle mine, rather than enjoying another sojourn at Her Majesty's Pleasure. She wasn't so easily fooled, but never let on.

"How many times is it now that you've been away on one of these work trips?" asked Sid, with a huge grin.

"Three, and it don't get any easier, although the food this time was a bit better. It's always nice to get back to my old caravan, because I miss my old dog and have to haul over to Langbridge, to get her back from cousin Mary."

Nozzer is what is kindly referred to as a general dealer, but less kindly could be described as a misfit living in the corner of a field, surrounded by the remains of old cars and other machinery, which he cannibalises for parts for anyone trying to keep an ancient car roadworthy.

"Did you get the bus over today?" asked Sid. "No, course not," said laughing Nozzer, "You know I don't hold with catching buses, blasted unreliable things. I drove."

Sid had known, the moment he asked the question, what the answer would be, because Nozzer simply could not resist the temptation to get behind the wheel, any wheel. Nozzer had also never been tempted to acquire tax or insurance for the old bangers he drove, and MOT certificates were similarly unknown to him.

The result was regular appearances before the magistrates in Malbury and too-frequent excursions to the treacle mine.

"I was on my way in here for a swift one. Fancy joining me?" asked Sid, and with that they disappeared through the door of the King's Head.

"Hello, Nozzer, long time no see. Have you come over to see your mum?" asked Peggy the barmaid. "I saw her in the bakers last week, she said you'd been down the treacle mine again."

"You're looking even more beautiful than last time I saw you, and that's saying something, Peggy love," said Nozzer as Peggy put the second pint of Old Todger down on the bar. "You'll have to visit me at my country estate some time, and enjoy a bottle of light ale, but if you want grub you'll have to bring it yourself."

"Are you still living in that scrapyard?" asked Peggy. "Not so much of the scrapyard, you cheeky beggar, that's my classic car parts supply business." replied Nozzer, with a huge grin.

The fledgeling conversation was cut short by the arrival of Sid's brother Joe, in work overalls whose white-splashed condition demonstrated to all that Joe had spent his morning plastering a ceiling.

"Nozzer, just the man I need to see. I need a halfshaft for the Cresta, and I'm hoping you can help. Yes please, a pint and bag of scratchings over here, Peggy love."

Joe's 1958 Vauxhall Cresta was his pride and joy. He had been restoring the car, which he described as "a right beauty", for the past three years, and kept promising that it was nearly finished, although those invited into the old shed where work was in progress were never really convinced.

There was a hint of glazed eyes as Joe relayed at length to Nozzer and Sid a step-by-step guide to Vauxhall Cresta restoration. "Just wait until I get her on the road, you'll all want a ride then, and so will you, won't you, Peggy love."

"I don't think so, Joe, I like a bit of comfort when I accept a lift from a gentleman. But then, I'm not sure you're always a gentleman."

Peggy was still laughing when Pc Nicholls walked in. "Is that your white Ford Sierra in the pub car park, Mr Grey, as if I really need to ask?"

"I'm not sure, officer, I did have a white Sierra stolen from my classic car parts business yesterday, but it was just one I was about to break up for spares, and not worth worrying about," said Nozzer, spluttering into his pint. "And you say you've found it – that's lucky then. I always say that you boys in blue are worth your weight in gold. Of course, it might not be mine."

"I wonder how it got from your scrapyard to the King's Head. Is it just a coincidence that you're here as well?" asked a bemused Pc Nicholls. "I'm going to do some checks, so don't go away, because I will be back."

"You don't look too worried, Nozzer," said Joe. "I'm not, because that car in the car park is not in my name. I never told the DVLA when I got it. They're the last people I want to know my business."

When Pc Nicholls re-appeared it was with the news that the Sierra had been declared SORN – permanently off the road – by the previous owner. "If it's yours, Mr Grey, get it removed, on a trailer, and back to your scrapyard. If anyone should be daft enough to drive it, we will throw the book at them."

"He's got to catch me first," said Nozzer as the policeman went back to his car. "Bit keen, your local copper, ain't he? He nicked me once for buying a few bits of lead. How was I to know it had come off a roof? That's the trouble today, nobody believes you. Every time I meet a copper he thinks I'm lying to him."

"That's because you are, you've never been known to tell a copper the truth," said Joe in a loud voice that started everyone in the bar laughing.

"Anyway, who's for another pint?" said Nozzer. "Three more over here, please, Peggy love."

With that the trio, Nozzer, Joe and Sid, settled down to some serious drinking, with Nozzer regaling his companions with tales of life down the fabled treacle mine.

"Does your mum really believe in your treacle mine story?" asked Sid. "Course she don't, but she thinks I think she believes it, and that keeps everyone happy," said Nozzer.

Pint followed pint and, by the time Peggy barked: "Come on you lucky lads, haven't you got homes to go to?" the trio were very, very drunk.

They staggered out of the pub, with Sid and Joe questioning Nozzer about how he was going to get home at that time of night, as they followed him across the car park.

"You can't do it, Nozzer, you'll end up nicked again," said Joe as Nozzer slipped behind the wheel of the Sierra and started it up. "You just watch me. You know I don't catch buses. Goodnight boys, it's been great to see you, and don't worry about me, I'll get home safely."

Joe and Sid looked on in amazement as Nozzer roared and clattered out of the car park and headed off along the main road in a cloud of smoke. They were even more amazed to hear the sound of a police car's siren.

"Oh dear, looks like another trip to the treacle mine," said Sid as he and Joe staggered off into the darkness.

Chapter 11

The Walking Lady

She was known to everyone in Little Bardon as The Walking Lady, striding briskly along the main street with monotonous regularity twice a day.

She walked everywhere, was never seen driving, nor on a bicycle, and never on a bus, not that any buses went within a mile of her cottage at the end of a long, unmade road separated from the seawall by just a field and a very deep ditch.

She always smiled and waved, always looked supremely happy, but seldom exchanged more than a few words as she strode purposefully on, always in a sheepskin coat and at least one scarf, no matter what the time of day, and whatever the weather.

"She's a rum 'un, that old girl," said Joe's brother Sid to his wife Marjorie. "I just can't fathom her at all. She's always trotting along, in her own little world.

"There's me out there working in the garden, just in me vest, and she's trotting past wearing that heavy coat and scarf. Barmy, if you ask me."

Of course, nobody did ask Sid, certainly not Marjorie, who called him a 'self-opinionated pillock', although only to her sister Joyce.

The Walking Lady had been a regular daily sight in the village for a couple of months when speculation gathered pace in the public bar of the King's Head about who this mystery woman was and why she was always walking.

"My mate Brian said he's started seeing her walking over Malbury way, and that's six miles from here," said Young Fred. "He reckons she's the woman who was in the papers a few weeks ago saying she's going to do some long walk for charity."

"Cobblers," said Dennis. "She's too old for that lark. I reckon she's just bonkers, if you ask me."

"We didn't ask you, and get your teeth off the bar and back into your mouth," said Peggy the barmaid, who had been transfixed on the scintillating conversation.

"Sorry, Peggy love, I took them out to eat my pork scratchings."

"You had peas for your dinner, didn't you, Dennis," said Young Fred.

"How on earth did you know that?" asked a bemused Dennis.

"Because the peas are still stuck to them. Just get them back in your mouth," said Peggy, sliding her ample bosom off the polished bar top.

Dennis gave his teeth a good swill in his beer glass and pushed them back into his mouth, watched in horror by Young Fred and the handful of locals spread along the bar.

"You're not going to drink that, are you?" said an amazed Young Fred, as Dennis answered by lifting his pint and draining it, followed by one of his familiar – some say far too familiar – loud belches.

"Another pint, please, Peggy love, and a fill-up for Young Fred, even if he is a cheeky so and so."

The subject of The Walking Lady slipped off the agenda, in favour of an earnest discussion about the merits of garden peas versus the mushy variety. Garden peas won the popular vote, but only after some heated discussion including an astute observation from Norman the vegetable king that mushy peas have obviously had all the goodness taken out.

However, the subject of The Walking Lady was back on the agenda a few days later.

"You'll never guess who's in the saloon bar," said Peggy. "The woman you call The Walking Lady, who's always marching through the village, and she certainly scrubs up well. She's with the vicar."

As a man, Dennis, Young Fred and Norman sidled to the end of the bar so they could get a view through to the saloon area.

"Well, I'll be blowed," said Norman, when he returned to the well-worn bar stool that had been his home for the evening. "She looks half presentable. Course, not up to your standard, Peggy, love. Another pint, when you're ready, and a bag of scratchings, of course."

He was in mid-slurp when the Reverend Stollery and the Walking Lady made an appearance in the public bar. "Gentlemen, I would like to introduce you to a very dear friend of mine, Mrs Mary Green, whom I am sure you have seen on her perambulations through the village."

There were assorted grunts and nods along the bar as the assembled throng looked the smiling woman over, hanging tightly to the vicar's arm."

"Mrs Green, who is of course a widow, and I have been friends for a number of years. Her late husband and I were at school together, and Mary, Mrs Green, is now living in the district, as you are doubtless aware, and has become something of a long distance walker, training to walk the 82 miles of the Essex Way, and doing it in the most arduous of fashions, with heavy clothing to help her acclimatise to the rigours of walking in summer heat."

"Good on yer, missus," said Norman, who had never been known for an enthusiasm for walking, nor for any other form of exercise that didn't involve throwing a dart or lifting a pint glass.

"It's about time the vicar got himself a woman, he's been here eight or nine years and that's the first we've seen," said Sid, as Reverend Stollery and Mary Green exited the pub and turned left, in the direction of the vicarage.

"It's been lovely to have met you all, and I am so sorry to drag Nigel away," she said as they disappeared out of the door.

"He's a sly 'un, and no mistake," said Norman. "Another pint and a bag of scratchings over here, please, Peggy love, and what do you think of the vicar's fancy woman?"

"There's no need to be rude, Norman, she seems a very nice lady. Good luck to him if he's found a nice lady friend," said Peggy, with the slightly disgruntled look that told those lined up along the public bar to mind what they said.

"I agree, Peggy love. Good luck to him, he's not a bad bloke, for a holy man," said Dennis, who hadn't been inside St Stephen's Church since his niece Pauline married there several years ago.

"I hope the vicar remembers the Ten Commandments," said Norman. "I wouldn't like to think he's doing anything he shouldn't."

When the laughter had died down, Young Fred piped up with "Doing what?" which started the laughter off again, and left Young Fred with a totally baffled look on his face.

The Walking Lady continued with her daily rambles through the village, although with a seemingly livelier step and with cheerier waves to those she passed.

"I reckon her and the vicar are a bit closer than just old friends; new friends, I reckon, and close ones at that," Norman confided to Peggy one Saturday lunchtime, as he mulled over whether he ought to have another bag of pork scratchings, his fourth, or whether to switch to dry roasted peanuts this time.

"Another pint and another bag of scratchings, please, Peggy love. What do you reckon about the old vicar and his lady friend, do you reckon they're, you know?"

"I know what, exactly? Stop winking. It's not my business, Norman, and it's not yours or anyone else's, now change the subject, and leave them in peace," said Peggy.

"I was just wondering if he takes his dog collar off before, you know," said Norman, chewing on another pork scratching.

Peggy shut down any possible further conversation on the topic of the vicar and The Walking Lady with an icy stare that left Norman in no doubt that he had overstepped the mark yet again and needed to shut up.

Then an excited Young Fred fairly leapt through the door, bursting with news. "You'll never guess what I just saw. I went to Malbury to get my mum's dry cleaning and bumped into the vicar and his lady friend looking in the jeweller's window."

"They're allowed to look in shop windows, it's not a crime," said Peggy, trying to sound uninterested, but desperate to know more.

"Yes, but when I walked back up the high street half an hour later they were coming out of the shop and she was holding his hand."

Well, that was enough to set the village rumour mill in motion, to give Peggy one of her frequent hot flushes and to make Young Fred the centre of attention for everyone in the bar, and in the saloon bar, too, because he couldn't resist dashing in there to share the news.

As luck would have it, the saloon bar patrons that Saturday lunchtime included two of the most accomplished gossips known to man, Mrs Davis and Mrs Ferguson, enjoying a small sherry as they awaited any juicy morsel of information, private or personal, that came their way.

Young Fred's revelation set both hearts thumping and mouths moving at double speed as they guessed, speculated and invented, then the mobile phones came out and whispered conversations conveyed the earth-shattering news to Mrs Gill, Iris the postwoman and Mrs Barnes, who passed it on via a sort of gossiping pyramid.

On any other Sunday, St Stephen's would welcome no more than a dozen to morning service, but this Sunday was different, very different, with 27 in the pews desperate to hear the news they were certain the vicar would share.

Mrs Davis, resplendent in one of her collection of Sunday hats, was one of the regular dozen, but Mrs Ferguson was an infrequent visitor and hatless Mrs Barnes only saw the inside of St Stephen's at Midnight Mass at Christmas.

Today, the trio of gossips and the friends who had gone with them, were united in their quest for news that would give them something to chew over for months to come.

"Have you noticed who is in the front pew?" Mrs Ferguson whispered to Iris the postwoman, sitting directly in front of her. "Yes, and doesn't she look smart. They make a lovely couple," Iris whispered back.

As Sunday services go, it could probably best be described as dull, and possibly a little sluggish, until the vicar invited The Walking Lady to stand beside him at the front; excitement mounted and reached boiling point when he said he had some news to impart.

"Mrs Green is going to walk The Essex Way, in stages, to raise money for the St Stephen's Fabric Fund, so if you could help by distributing sponsorship forms, that would be greatly appreciated," said the vicar.

"Is that it?" asked Mrs Davis. "Isn't there any other news today?" There were glum faces when he shook his head, and Mrs Barnes confided to her colleagues that she wouldn't have bothered coming if she had known, and she certainly wouldn't have sat so close to elderly Mr Barrett, who was well known in the village for his extreme flatulence, which had once earned him a ban from the bakery.

As they all rose and turned to leave the pews, The Walking Lady nudged the vicar; he gave a cough and said: "My apologies, Mrs Green, Mary, has reminded me of the most important news of the day."

The whole church froze, and heads swivelled to look at the couple at the front. "Yes, there will be a jumble sale in the church hall next Saturday."

There was a deathly silence, and a look from The Walking Lady towards the vicar that could have stopped an elephant in its tracks.

"Ah, yes, as I suspect some of you will have already guessed, especially since we bumped into a young man from the village when we visited a certain shop in Malbury, Mary and I are to be married, here in St Stephen's, later in the year. We hope you will all approve and be happy for us," said the smiling vicar, tightly clutching the arm of his beaming bride-to-be.

"At last, something interesting in this village," said a delighted Mrs Barnes, as she raced, phone in hand, to beat gossip-desperate Mrs Ferguson to the door.

Chapter 12

Ghostly Goings-On

It started with a chance remark over a pint or three in the public bar of the King's Head, and ended with Norman, that stoic ex-coalman and Little Bardon's undisputed vegetable king, doubting his sanity.

"I was talking to old Bill from Greenacres today, and he was saying about the old ghost on the seawall," said Joe, as he pushed his empty pint glass across the bar top. "Another one in here, please, Peggy love, and another bag of scratchings."

"What was he saying?" asked his brother Sid. "He was saying that the old Roman is seen on the seawall about now, the beginning of February. He hasn't seen the ghost himself, but said his dad saw it and reckoned it was definitely a Roman soldier."

The legend of the ghostly Roman soldier marching across the top of the seawall, from the direction of the fort that was now just a preserved collection of stones, was well known in the village, but it had generally been regarded as a made-up story to frighten the gullible.

But gullible or not, it set Joe thinking: "It might be a good laugh to go ghost hunting. We could have a few in here on Saturday night, then have a walk down Grange Road to the seawall and see if that old Roman is about."

By this time Norman had joined the conversation, and was quick to chip in with "I'm up for that, Joe, it might be a bit of fun. It's going to be cold, mind, so we'll need a bottle of something to warm us up."

And so, on Saturday night, Joe, Sid and Norman supped their usual four or five pints, stocked up on supplies – "half a dozen bags of scratchings, please, Peggy love," – and when Peggy called out her familiar "Come on, you lucky lads, haven't you got homes to go to?" those intrepid ghost hunters pulled on coats and hats and headed out into the cold.

But during the evening, as talk of ghost hunting gathered pace, Dennis and Young Fred had started planning their own evening's entertainment. "We'll put the wind up those old boys tonight, Peggy love. We're going to have a creep about down the sea wall and give them a bit of a fright."

"I've got the whisky," said Norman, patting his coat pocket as the trio walked away from the village street, down Grange Road in pitch darkness and bitter cold. "And I've got the scratchings," said Sid, "but I'm not so sure this is a good idea tonight, it's blasted cold. My hands are already frozen, and there's a flake or two of snow in the air."

Just as he said that, they saw a dark shape in the distance, then a second one. "Oh, I don't believe this, the old Roman's brought reinforcements," said Joe, with a definite quiver in his voice.

"Hello boys, what are you up to?" said a voice out of the darkness. There was a collective sigh of relief from the trio when they realised it was just Waggy and Podge, on their way home from one of their regular poaching expeditions.

'You haven't seen the copper about tonight, have you? We don't want to bump into him, he might want a look in our bags. We don't normally see you old boys out like this. Did you get chucked out of the pub?" asked Waggy, who was otherwise best known in Little Bardon as the local tree surgeon.

Norman said no, there was no special reason for them being out, they just wanted a nice walk, and with that they continued towards the seawall.

They stood under the lee of a concrete pillbox, one of those wartime structures used by soldiers guarding the coast. This one was on the seaward side of the wall, directly in line with the worst weather the North Sea could throw at it, and that night it threw plenty.

It was bitterly cold and starting to snow harder and harder, with the snow blowing directly into their faces. Even swigs of whisky and two bags of scratchings each did nothing to keep out the cold; it was eerily quiet with only the occasional belch and Joe's flatulence to break the monotony. "Sorry boys, I knew I shouldn't have had that curry tonight," said a laughing Joe.

"Three pickled eggs in the pub didn't help, either," said Norman, looking at his watch: "It's gone midnight, I reckon we should head back."

And so they did, starting a whisky-aided stagger through swirling snow in the bitter cold, but they had only got a few yards when Norman turned back towards the seawall and gasped as he saw the hazy, indistinct figure of what looked like a Roman soldier marching silently through the driving snow, but in an instant it was gone.

Joe and Sid were a few yards ahead when they realised Norman was not with them. "Come on Norman," said Joe, thrusting his hands deeper into his pockets to try to keep warm. "What are you doing, standing there like a spare whatsit at a wedding?"

"I saw him, that old Roman, he was there, clear as you like. It was him, marching through the snow. He had his helmet on and everything, and he was wearing a sort of skirt."

"Oh yeah, right, how come we didn't see him, then?" said Joe. "But I did," said Sid. "As I turned I just saw him for a second as he disappeared. I definitely saw him. I don't like this, I'm going home."

They walked back along Grange Road in swirling snow, total darkness and complete silence that was only broken when they reached the village street and exchanged goodnights as they headed to bed.

Norman didn't sleep well that night, unable to get the vision of the Roman out of his head. He had seen the soldier so clearly, albeit for only a second or two. And Sid said he had seen him, as well, so it was real, he wasn't dreaming, it wasn't his imagination, thought Norman, as his befuddled brain worked out what on earth had happened.

His parting words to Joe and Sid last night had been a mumbled invitation to their usual Sunday lunchtime pint, and so he headed to the King's Head at midday, where Peggy met him with a cheery "Have a nice night down the sea wall, did you? Did you see your ghost?"

"I don't want to talk about it if you don't mind, Peggy love. Pint and a bag of scratchings, please."

That was when Joe and Sid walked in, and Joe called out: "You'll never believe it, Peggy love, this pair reckon they saw the old Roman out on the wall last night. I reckon it was the whisky talking."

Norman was uncharacteristically quiet, in fact he looked as if his mind was definitely somewhere else. "I don't want to talk about last night," he said.

"You silly old sods," said Peggy, "It was a wind-up. It was Young Fred and Dennis messing you about. You didn't really think you'd seen a ghost, did you? I knew you were daft, you lot, but this beats everything."

Norman felt a sense of relief that it wasn't really a ghost, but at the same time he was annoyed that Dennis and Young Fred had made a fool of him, and he told them so when they made an appearance a few minutes later.

"But it wasn't us, we thought about having a laugh, but when it started to snow Young Fred said he was going home to bed, and I did the same," said Dennis.

"Another pint and a bag of scratchings, when you're ready, Peggy love," said an ashen-faced Norman, who took them to a seat in the corner of the bar and didn't say another word all lunchtime.

Chapter 13

Good Old Percy

Percy had been an evening fixture in the corner of the King's Head public bar, nursing a nightly glass or two of barley wine, since time immemorial; at least, that's how it felt.

At seven on the dot every evening, come rain or shine, Percy and his little dog Tiny appeared, took up station in the corner seat and took delivery of a bottle of barley wine.

At eight, Percy took his leave and went home to wife Mabel, with warmed slippers and an hour in front of the television before the early night that every octogenarian has earned.

And so it had been, every evening without fail, for more years than anyone in Little Bardon could really remember.

"Just how long has Percy been coming in here? He hasn't missed a night in all the years I've been working here," said barmaid Peggy one night to the darts team straggled along the bar.

"Longer than me, Peggy love, and that's saying something. I've been a regular for over 40 years," said long-retired Norman, who used to build up a thirst humping hundredweight sacks of coal on and off the Co-op coal lorry. "And do you know, he told me the other day he's going to be 90 in a few weeks. Another pint over here, please, Peggy love, and another bag of scratchings."

"Oh bless him, he's doing well," said Peggy. "Can anyone find out when his birthday is? We ought to help him celebrate." "Leave it to us,

Peggy love. And I'd better have another pint and a bag of scratchings, while you're there. Percy's always been part of this pub, so we certainly ought to do something. Can't imagine coming in here early evening and not seeing him," said Sid, whose imagination started to run riot at the thought of such a good excuse for yet another boozy evening.

A couple of days later, he had important news. He had popped in to see Mabel and found out that the magic birthday was just ten days away, but she had confided that she was worried about Percy's health, which was not bad enough to stop his nightly excursions for a barley wine, but worrying nonetheless.

With Peggy's gentle guiding hand the public bar regulars started planning Percy's surprise birthday evening. "And we can all chip in for a present for him, though I ain't got a clue what," said Dennis. "If he smoked I could get a load of cheap fags, but he don't smoke, so that's no good."

"What about one of them kissograms, although I don't suppose she'd be a patch on you, Peggy love, oh, and another pint over here, and one for dad," said Young Fred. "And a bag of scratchings," said Fred senior.

The suggestions came thick and fast, becoming more and more absurd as the pints of Old Todger flowed. A tandem skydive was quickly ruled out, as was swimming with dolphins, and a hot air balloon flight was a definite no-no for a 90-year-old, as was Young Fred's suggestion of a trip to Amsterdam's red light district.

"You really are a dozy bunch, with your stupid ideas," said Peggy, "let's just keep it simple, invite his daughter and family, lay on some food and make a fuss of him."

"I like that idea, Peggy love, and I'm sure my mate Mick what does the wedding cars will pick him up in his Rolls Royce and bring him here, if I stand him a couple of pints," said Young Fred.

"Make sure he takes the white ribbons off, otherwise Percy might think his luck's changed," laughed Dennis.

Mick was as good as Young Fred's word, and the Rolls Royce Silver Shadow purred the 150 yards from Percy's old people's bungalow to deposit him and Mabel to the pub with its Happy Brithday banner made by Young Fred, who had never mastered the art of spelling.

The public bar was packed, and erupted in cheers and clapping as Percy, Mabel and Percy's constant companion Tiny, were ushered through the door; Charlie the landlord had even put on a tie for such a special event and Peggy was in the lacy top she kept for special occasions.

Percy had never looked happier, although Mabel confided to Peggy that she had had serious doubts that Percy would be fit enough to come along, "but he was determined to get here as his friends had made such an effort for him. He's always been a tough old sod."

Happy Percy was soon working his way through Charlie's stock of barley wine, and tucking into salmon sandwiches and sausage rolls, serenaded by Fred senior, whose tuneless dirges got louder the more drunk he became, until Peggy finally told him: "Fred, shut up or go home."

"Sorry, Peggy love, only trying to cheer him up," said bleary-eyed Fred.

"Percy don't need cheering up, he needs a bit of help standing up; he wants to say something," said Dennis.

They helped visibly tipsy Percy to his feet, Dennis on one side and Sid on the other, and he told the now silent bar: "This is the best birthday ever. Thank you everyone for making it so special, and thank you Mabel for making the last 66 years so special."

Mabel wiped away some tears as she rose and gave her man a big hug, then sat down with him as the evening got into full swing.

"Two pints over here, please, Peggy love, and a bag of scratchings," said Joe. "Same over here, Peggy love," called out Norman, "and whatever Percy and Mabel are drinking."

Mabel gave Percy's hand a squeeze, then called Norman over and whispered: "I don't think he's going to want another one, where he is now."

Suddenly the pub went quiet, and all eyes were on Percy, sitting in his favourite corner of the bar, with a glass of barley wine in front of him, a huge smile on his face, Mabel's hand in his and his faithful dog Tiny curled up on his lap.

"What a way to go," said Peggy. "Good old Percy."

Chapter 14

The Romany

They had barely set up camp when a haughty woman stuck her head out of the window of a Range Rover and shouted: "And what do you think you lot are doing? This is private land, so be off with you."

"Begging your pardon, ma'am, but we're here for a couple of nights, then we'll be moving on," said the younger of the two men, as he finished putting out a water bucket for the horse.

"We'll see about that, and see what the policeman has to say," said an irate Mrs Nixon-Smith, who is universally referred to in the public bar of the King's Head as "that snooty cow from Glebe."

She had arrived in Little Bardon two years ago, and since then had done nothing to endear herself to villagers. In fact, she had gone out of her way to antagonise, belittle and generally make herself thoroughly unpopular with the locals.

Mrs Nixon-Smith, whose downtrodden husband left elegant Glebe House early every morning to catch the train from Malbury for a job in the City, was universally disliked, except by the equally obnoxious Major Dobson, chairman of the parish council, and by just a handful of others who regard themselves as being in the upper strata of village society.

Unfortunately for Pc Nicholls, the irate woman spotted him as he came out of the bakery with his mid-morning snack of a tuna baguette, two doughnuts and a coffee, and proceeded to spoil his quiet morning, with a tirade about "damned gipsies in Pullhams Lane. I want them moved on, and moved on now."

"Don't upset yourself so much, madam, I'll go and see them," said the young policeman. "Don't just see them, move them, we don't want their sort in our village. This is a respectable village, we don't want gipsies camped in the lane. Who knows what crimes they will commit."

By the time Pc Nicholls arrived at the greensward at the end of Pullhams Lane there was quite a gathering, laughing, joking and slapping one another on the back in an obvious show of bonhomie from a group gathered round a beautifully painted traditional 'barrel top' Romany caravan

"Pc Nicholls, I would like you to meet a very old and very dear friend who I have not seen for a long, long time," said Reggie Naylor, who farms at Great Wick.

"Daniel and his wife Rose used to visit us every year to help with the fieldwork, but he gave up travelling, how many years ago, Daniel?"

"Thirty years, almost to the day, since I was on the road, and I have missed it every day since," said the frail-looking man, who supported himself on a stick.

"Father stopped travelling when my mother became very ill, and now he's ill himself, which is why we are here," said the younger man. "He wanted one last visit to some of the atchin tans, the traditional Romany stopping places, where he and my late mother spent time every year.

The younger man was Michael, Daniel's son, who explained that he was spending part of the six weeks summer holiday from teaching to make his father's dream come true; Daniel's advanced cancer meant this would be the last opportunity to do that.

Daniel had spent months painting and refurbishing the gipsy caravan that had been standing outside the bungalow that had been his home for 30 years.

Rose had been dead for many years, and Daniel knew that his time was approaching; the diagnosis last year had not been good, but he accepted that he had had a good life and it would soon be time to meet his beloved Rose again.

When the travelling stopped, Michael was ten years old, and a very bright boy. Rose had told Daniel that her abiding wish was for Michael to have a good education and to make a future away from the harsh Romany travelling life.

Daniel promised her that he would, and the proof that he kept that promise was that Michael was now head of year at a comprehensive school, not many miles from where Daniel lived.

When Daniel told him that he wanted to visit some of the old traditional stopping places, Michael set about making that dream come true. They chose three places, this one in Pullhams Lane, another the other side of Malbury and a third in the north of the county.

"I knew we couldn't drive a horse and wagon on busy roads, so my cousin Lee with his horsebox and trailer is dropping us off at the outskirts of each place and picking us up a couple of days later. Luckily, we have been able to borrow one of Lee's horses, and a phone call to dad's dear old friend Reggie means we have food for the horse waiting at each stop."

"Pc Nicholls," said Daniel, turning to the policeman. "You're not Charlie Nicholls' boy, are you?" When he nodded, the old man said: "He was a proper village copper, your dad, very firm, mind, but always fair. He never did us any harm. Reggie told me he had passed, I was sorry to hear it."

Michael said he and his father planned to stay for two days before moving on to the second stopping place; they planned to cook outside in the traditional way – something his father had not done for many years – and to spend their evenings around the camp fire with some of Daniel's old friends.

"I think that's a wonderful idea. I would love to join you later, when I am off duty, if I may, to hear a bit more about my dad," said Pc Nicholls. "I will let my inspector know you are staying a while."

The other old friends who had joined Daniel, Michael and Reggie on that scrap of grass verge all said they would be back in the evening to re-live old memories and make some new ones.

And so they did, and the food they brought with them was soon cooking over the open fire under a full moon and sky full of stars. The fire crackled, the laughter around it was infectious and the anecdotes exchanged were compelling listening.

Then the Range Rover pulled up, the window went down and Mrs Nixon-Smith said: "I really don't believe you people are still here, and you should be ashamed of yourself, Pc Nicholls, consorting with law breakers. I am going to report you"

Pc Nicholls rose from his perch on a plastic box beside the fire, walked over to the car and said: "Firstly, Mrs Nixon-Smith, these gentlemen are not breaking any law. Secondly, please feel free to report me for enjoying an evening off duty with visitors to the village, and visitors I am proud to call my friends. If there is nothing else I can help you with, I will get back to those friends. Have a nice evening, ma'am."

"You really are Charlie Nicholls' boy, I can see that. He would have handled that in the same way," said Daniel. Michael shook the young policeman's hand and whispered "Thank you."

The evening ended with a final story or two shared over the dying embers of the fire and then warm handshakes and back slaps as the hosts and visitors parted ways.

"I'll pop by in the morning, to see if you need anything," said Pc Nicholls as he made his way into the night.

Michael walked slowly across to the police car when it drew up next morning, and Pc Nicholls knew from his face that bad news was about to come.

"I think you've guessed what I am going to say; sadly, dad passed in the night. He said he knew he was going to see his Rose again soon, then slipped peacefully away.

"He spent his last hours in a place he loved all those years ago, and among old and new friends. Who can ask for more than that."

Chapter 15

Mayday Mayhem

The idea was undoubtedly a good one, and so it should have been, coming as it did from Mrs Gladman, esteemed chairperson of the Little Bardon Women's Institute, and holder of the same lofty position in St Stephen's Mothers' Union.

Mrs Gladman was what could fairly be described as a doer, someone who steams into every job to get it done, and who sweeps all and sundry along with her, whether they like it or not. And she is definitely someone who likes to call the tune.

"Ladies, I would like your support for an event involving the whole village," she told the WI's January meeting. "A Mayday festival on the village green, so come along ladies, chop chop, let's get our thinking caps on."

"Another one of her big ideas that never come to nothing," whispered Mrs Barnes to Miss Smith. "She'll have us dancing round the blasted maypole next."

"One thought," said Mrs Gladman, as Mrs Ferguson got up from her seat to switch on the tea urn, "a refreshment tent, and a maypole."

"That's two thoughts already," whispered Mrs Barnes, "and she ain't started yet."

Miss Day, who had spent her working life teaching at St Michael's Primary in Malbury, volunteered to organise something for the village children, and others said they would be happy to help in any way they could, so long as no organising was involved.

Iris the postwoman had a friend who danced with the Malbury morris side, so she would ask if they would come along to give a display, and several of the ladies thought they could persuade grumpy Mrs Cotton to bring along some of her ponies to give rides.

Then the newest member of the WI piped up: "I have considerable experience of organising such events, from when I lived in Surbiton, so I am happy to chair a Mayday Festival committee," said Mrs Nixon-Smith.

"It is very kind of you to offer," said Mrs Gladman, bristling with indignation, "but I think the festival organisation should rest in the hands of the WI committee, of which I, of course, am chairperson."

To say that Mrs Nixon-Smith was miffed is a gross understatement. She was not used to being anything but in charge, it simply wasn't in her nature to accept second place in anything.

"I need to leave," she said, "I have an important appointment." "You don't want your tea, then," Mrs Ferguson called after her as Mrs Nixon-Smith disappeared at considerable speed through the door.

"Are we agreed then that I should set up and chair the committee? There being no nays, I will take that as your approval. So let us all put our thinking caps on, ladies, and come up with ideas, and I take it you will all happily serve on the committee, if so asked," said Mrs Gladman, calling the business part of the WI meeting to a close.

The event gradually took shape over the next few weeks and, by the WI's March meeting, there was plenty to report, including that Mrs Nixon-Smith had objected to Major Dobson, the parish council chairman, about the village green being the proposed venue.

It was, she had insisted, wholly inappropriate for music and dancing to be allowed on a public space where she was planning a picnic for old friends from Surbiton. Major Dobson, despite being known locally as Major Miseryguts, had given her short shrift and told her the festival was being held with the parish council's blessing.

There was a yes from Malbury Morris, reported Iris the postwoman, Mrs Cotton was happy to bring along her ponies, Mrs Ferguson was already recruiting volunteers for the tea tent, Waggy the tree surgeon could supply a maypole and Miss Day had great plans for activities for the village children.

The Mayday Festival poster that was put up in the King's Head caused quite a stir. "What the heck is Welly Wanging?" asked Young Fred. "You have to see how far you can chuck a welly," said Sid, who was more interested in the Yard of Ale contest, and the possibility for a rematch with his brother Joe, who had downed a yard two seconds faster than him when they went head to head a few Christmases ago.

"I'll have to get in some practice. Another pint and bag of scratchings, please, Peggy love."

"I reckon you'll have a fair bit of competition from those morris men," said Norman. "They might dance around waving hankies and jingling bells like a bunch of fairies, but by heck they can down the pints.

"They're all beards and beerguts. They only do the dancing to build up a thirst. Oh, and I've told that old Mrs Gladman that the darts team will help out on the day. I reckon we can run the Yard of Ale."

Organisation reached fever pitch during April, with people all round the village recruited by the forceful Mrs Gladman, whether they were keen or not.

Mayday dawned with a beautiful blue sky, a warm breeze, and chaos on the village green. Pc Nicholls had been out at 7am to put out cones to stop parking on the roadside, Waggy had arrived about the same time with the ribbon-bedecked maypole and Mrs Gladman was in a panic after mislaying her clipboard with its meticulously drawn plans and instruction sheets.

By 10am, people were arriving to set up stalls, but it was to little avail because Mrs Gladman was nowhere to be seen and no-one knew where anything should go – except Mrs Nixon-Smith, who had picked up the clipboard laying next to Mrs Gladman's car when she took her spaniels for an early morning walk, and had 'forgotten' to hand it back.

Fortunately, Mrs Gladman was back on the village green by 10.30 after printing off all the plans and information sheets again at home.

"About time, missus, we've got a lot to do before it starts," said Fred senior, who along with his son Young Fred, had been enrolled as one of Mrs Gladman's coterie of stewards.

"Oh dear, yes, yes, time is our enemy, we must get on, chop chop," said an exasperated Mrs Gladman, desperately trying to marshal people and cars, as chaos continued to reign.

Mrs Nixon-Smith found it extremely difficult to stop herself laughing out loud as she walked her spaniels past the village green for the second time that morning. Serves the old bat right, she thought.

But miraculously, by midday, stalls had been set out, the maypole was ready, Young Fred's attempt at a PA system had been set up and tested and a rudimentary arena had been marked out with stakes and rope.

Larry, from Larry's Lavs at Danford, had arrived with portable ladies' and gents' toilets and Charlie from the King's Head had delivered the pub's Yard of Ale glass and a barrel of beer.

Mrs Gladman, reserve clipboard in hand, called her troops together and announced: "I think we are ready. I have scheduled the children's country dancing display for 2pm, morris dancing at three, Welly Wanging at four and the Yard of Ale for whenever the darts team can get here."

It was the calm before the storm.

The official start time was one o' clock, and that is when the first problem arose, when Mrs Cotton's horsebox pulled on to the village green – an hour later than promised – and promptly got stuck, with wheels spinning on wet grass and Mrs Cotton braying that someone should have ensured a hard access point.

Fortunately, jovial Brian from Griffins Farm had been delivering bales of straw with his tractor and trailer and was able to pull the lorry out, but not without leaving a mess of splattered mud.

"If I'd known it was going to be like this, I would never have come," said grumpy Mrs Cotton, who was never one to smile.

"It's a pity she did, really," said Mrs Barnes as she helped Mrs Ferguson set up tables and chairs in the tea tent. "She was always a misery when she came in the bakery, and she hasn't changed. Oh, what's that?"

'That' was a dreadful squawking and high-pitched whistling coming out of the PA speakers set up on poles either side of the arena. "Just teething trouble, they were all right when I set up this morning," said a red-faced Young Fred, who had learned his sound engineering skills from a YouTube video and an old copy of Practical Wireless magazine. The terrible noises brought Mrs Gladman running over, reserve clipboard in hand and a look of panic on her face.

Young Fred had borrowed the sound equipment from his DJ mate Glenn in Malbury, with a promise that it would be returned intact by the end of the evening.

When Mrs Nixon-Smith went past on her third dog walk of the day she had fingers in ears and a huge grin, and it was at that point that one of the ponies went racing past, pursued by Mrs Cotton, who put on a surprising burst of speed for such a large lady.

By two o'clock, Mrs Gladman's nerves were jangling and tiny beads of perspiration dotted her forehead as she did her best to co-ordinate a hundred and one tasks. "Are your children ready, Miss Day?" she called, and yes, Miss Day gave a confident thumbs-up as she led the children in to the arena to begin their display.

Mrs Gladman's mood lightened a little when she saw the darts team approaching, ready for their task of organising the Yard of Ale competition, but it quickly darkened when it became obvious that they had spent their lunchtime in the King's Head and were somewhat the worse for wear.

As the children danced round the maypole, desperately trying to keep the ribbons from tangling and trying to avoid falling in a heap, two of the larger girls fell over and two dancing boys started throwing punches at each other.

And, not surprisingly, Joe and Dennis from the darts team were warming up for the Yard of Ale with a sample pint out of the barrel.

Meanwhile, the PA system continued to whistle and squawk, Mrs Ferguson and Mrs Barnes were arguing over who was in charge of the tea tent, and Mrs Gladman was panicking over the late arrival of the morris dancers.

Fred senior, the village's irrepressible but tuneless balladeer, started crooning into the PA system, much to the embarrassment of Young Fred – it was the first time anyone had heard 'The green, green grass of home' with accompanying whistles and squawks, and it was so bad that Fred senior won a round of applause.

Malbury Morris arrived, and it was a real eye-opener for the King's Head stalwarts, who were waiting for burly, bearded morris men to limber up with a turn at the Yard of Ale – they were all women, and none of them likely to down the two and a half pints that the yard glass held.

"I don't believe this," said Sid, "there's no men, it's all women." "Didn't you know it's an all-female morris side now? They can't recruit any men," said Iris the postwoman. "But one or two of them could drink you under the table."

The morris dancing was quite spectacular – traditional dancing with music played on concertina, fiddle and accordion – and went down really well with the crowd.

Then one of the dancers, Doreen, asked Sid: "Fancy your chances against me in the Yard of Ale, then? I'm told you're the best here today." It was like a red rag to a bull, and Sid confidently told brother Joe: "I'm going to hate making the girl look stupid, but it has to be done."

Surrounded by his darts team mates, and with a big, stupid grin on his face, Sid raised the glass and glugged down the beer in 32 seconds, to cheers and claps and chants of 'Champion' from the team.

He smiled as Doreen lifted the glass – and downed the full two and a half pints in 30 seconds, beating an astonished Sid by two seconds. Everyone went quiet, and a humbled Sid stood slowly shaking his head.

But it was nothing compared to the fiasco in the Welly Wanging – first the welly went missing and was found in the mouth of an exuberant Labrador racing around the green, then Molly the morris dancer out-threw everyone, including an enthusiastic Young Fred, to win the prize of a gallon of beer.

Then the heavens opened, rain ran in a torrent along the road next to the village green, Mrs Cotton's horsebox got stuck again, the PA system short-circuited, the tea tent collapsed, Mrs Nixon-Smith's posh picnic became a soggy mess and the ink on the paperwork on Mrs Gladman's reserve clipboard started to run.

Oh well, thought an exasperated Mrs Gladman as she pulled her foot out of a muddy puddle, it could have been worse, I suppose, as she overbalanced and ended up on her bottom in a huge puddle - although she really couldn't imagine how.

Chapter 16

A Night Best Forgotten

There are times that are best erased from the memory because they are so painful, so distressing, that only time will heal the wound caused, peel away the scar tissue and return you to a happy time.

The night the King's Head ran out of pork scratchings was one such painful time, and it will be remembered forever, engraved in the annals of Little Bardon's history, talked about whenever village stalwarts get together to sink a pint or throw a dart.

That unforgettable Friday night started as every other Friday night, with Norman, Sid, Dennis and Young Fred sinking their first pints of Old Todger and enjoying their first bags of scratchings.

Then the bombshell struck. "Another pint and another bag of scratchings, please, Peggy love," said Norman, preparing for a long evening of beer, darts and scratchings.

"Sorry, Norman, we've run out of scratchings, packet of cheese and onion do you instead?"

Peggy's words had a devastating effect; it was as if the world had suddenly stood still, there was silence where there had been a babble of happy voices, there were cries of "are you serious?" and "that must be a joke," and even Conrad with the tricky eye stopped playing the fruit machine, albeit momentarily.

"Are you having a laugh, Peggy love, you know Friday nights are not Friday nights without six pints and six bags of scratchings," said a visibly distraught Norman.

"Same for the rest of us," said Sid, who held the pub record for eating 12 bags of scratchings on a memorable Friday night which ended with him falling over the kerb on the way home and being sick in the ornamental planter lovingly installed on the edge of the village green by the WI. There were some who said, rather unkindly, that it was not wholly unexpected after drinking 12 pints of Old Todger and consuming an unspecified number of pickled eggs.

"Well, that's our evening ruined," said Dennis, who had no sympathy for Peggy's explanation that landlord Charlie had flu and had been unable to get to the cash and carry. "That's no excuse, he can't just run out of something like that. He should plan better."

"Truth is, we can't keep up with demand from you lot," said Peggy. "The cash and carry told Charlie a while back that no other pub gets through pork scratchings like we do. You'll just have to make do with crisps or peanuts, we've got plenty of cheese and onion and a few salt and vinegar. What's it to be?"

"I'm sorry, Peggy love, but I might have to take my custom elsewhere tonight, somewhere that caters for the drinking man who enjoys scratchings rather than poncey cheese and onion crisps," said Fred senior. "And I'll second that," said Conrad with the tricky eye during another momentary pause from hitting the buttons of the fruit machine.

"Where are you going, then, you daft sods? This is the only pub in the village, and I don't think even you lot would be daft enough to drive to the Feathers or one of the other pubs in Malbury, and risk getting nicked."

"Ah, but we could get a taxi, Peggy love, then we could get a bag of chips or a kebab on the way home. Anyone up for that?" asked Fred senior.

"You can keep your kebab, I'm not keen on foreign grub, and I'm certainly not chipping in for a taxi," replied Sid, and that seemed to be the general consensus from the discerning gourmets stretched along the bar.

"What about if Young Fred rides to the Feathers on his motorbike and buys a load of scratchings? He's still only half way through his first pint, so he can't get nicked," said Sid.

Young Fred reluctantly agreed, but then remembered he was almost out of petrol, so the plan was shelved. It was time for plan B, although no-one could actually think of a plan B, despite an outbreak of muttering and head scratching.

"I'll only eat a bag of cheese and onion crisps if I have a pickled egg with each one," said Norman, and that became plan B by popular vote, although only after Peggy checked that there were plenty of pickled eggs in the store cupboard.

"Two giant jars, plus the one under the bar, so you lot should be okay for the evening, and if you get through that lot, Heaven help us all," said Peggy.

"Another pint, Peggy love, bag of cheese and onion and a pickled egg," became the repeated order all along the bar. The first jar was quickly emptied, and the contents of the second one were disappearing fast when the problems started.

To say it was a touch whiffy, and more than a little noisy, is a gross understatement; in fact, there was a distinctly unpleasant aroma, a definite eggy smell that even worked its way through to the saloon bar, from where there were queries about the drains.

"Do you have to keep eating pickled eggs, can't you just leave it at beer and crisps?" implored Peggy, who by this time had donned a mask left over from the pandemic, and declared: "Covid was nowhere near as bad as this."

"Forget Covid, we've been denied our rights to enjoy a pint and a bag of scratchings. I can't eat cheese and onion crisps without a pickled egg, washed down with a pint. And I'd better have another pint here, Peggy love, these crisps are making my throat dry. I won't have crisps this time, though, I'll have two pickled eggs instead," said Norman.

Young Fred was the first to declare an end to egg consumption for the evening: "My poor old guts won't take any more. I think I've overdone it a bit." "Me as well," said Sid, looking decidedly queasy, which was very unusual for a man of such renowned eating habits. "I think it's reacting with the vindaloo my missus made for tea. She knows I hate that foreign muck, but keeps cooking weird stuff."

By this time the previously seemingly inexhaustible pickled egg supply had dried up anyway, and a jar of pickled onions had also been finished off, much to Peggy's relief as she looked across the bar at the clock on the wall.

"Come on, you lucky lads, haven't you got homes to go to? Oh, and by the way, Charlie has said he'll get off his sick bed to get to the cash and carry tomorrow for scratchings and a supply of air fresheners."

"And tell him, don't forget two big jars of pickled eggs," said Norman," I think we've all got quite a taste for them now."

"I think it might be time for me to retire," said Peggy.

Chapter 17

The Woo-Woo Club

"Is your mum coming to the clairvoyant evening tonight, Young Fred?" asked Peggy as she pushed his lunchtime pint of Old Todger across the King's Head bar.

"You mean the Woo-Woo Club; yes, she'll be there, she won't miss her monthly nutty night, as dad calls it."

"Why do you always call it the Woo-Woo Club?" asked Sid. "My missus reckons it's a good night out, although I'm glad it's held in the upstairs function room here, because it's not far to collect her and walk her home. She says she just goes for a laugh, but I think she believes a lot of the twaddle."

"Well," said Young Fred, "I would have thought it was pretty obvious why I call it the Woo-Woo Club – that's what ghosts say, they go woo-woo as they float about, I thought everyone knew that."

Little Bardon's monthly clairvoyant evenings had been running for a year, and had proved popular with the more open-minded members of village society – or the feeble-minded as Sid described them, although he was careful that his wife Marjorie never heard him say that.

There had been reports a few months ago that an orb had been seen floating around the room, and several people swore blind that they had been connected with long-dead loved ones.

But that was always pooh-poohed by the disbelievers in the public bar, who just thought it was a night out for anyone daft enough to believe in the supernatural.

"Tonight's going to be different – the clairvoyant who's coming along also does tarot card readings, so why don't you lot go along and see what the future holds," said a smiling Peggy.

"Some of you know the clairvoyant, Nozzer's old mum Norah. She's not done it here before, but they say she's got a real gift, a very good success rate at conjuring up spirits, and yes, Dennis, your pint and bag of scratchings are coming up," said Peggy, who had always avoided the clairvoyant evenings in case her late husband Don came through, asking for money, as he always did when he was alive. Peggy had often told people she had been glad to see the back of Don, who had an aversion to work, but excelled at scrounging off her.

"It's a pity Norah couldn't have conjured up someone to save Nozzer from another spell in the nick. He's back in for six months for the usual – too much to drink, no licence, no tax, no insurance, dodgy tyres and speeding," said Norman, who had joined the conversation after standing quietly drinking and thinking about his own ghostly experience a few months before.

"I don't want anything to do with ghosts, but I might try my luck with the tarot cards. Do you reckon they can help with numbers for the lottery?" he asked.

The plan was for a brief tarot session, to see if it was popular, followed by an evening of clairvoyance, if Norah had enough time for all of that – and enough energy. Norman, Dennis, Sid, Young Fred, Fred senior and Sid's brother Joe all said they would have a fiver's worth of tarot reading, because it would be a good laugh, if nothing else.

No-one was quite sure what to expect, although Norah certainly seemed to know what she was doing with the set of 78 tarot cards, explaining to Sid when she did his reading that the Fool card on the table in front of him was nothing personal, when he asked the cards the question "Should I retire?" but indicated that he was on the verge of an unexpected and exciting new adventure.

"That's it, I'm definitely going to retire, well, if I win the lottery I am. Is there anything in the cards about a lottery win?" Definitely not, said Norah, the cards gave an insight into the past, present and future, but nothing about winning the lottery.

Young Fred was excited when the Lovers card was produced, and asked if it meant he should ask Molly the young morris dancer who beat him in the welly wanging contest at the village's Mayday Festival, for a date.

"The card means there are major life-changing choices to make, but it is telling you to avoid temptation," Norah warned him, but Young Fred didn't take much notice of that because he had been tempted by thoughts of Molly ever since that Mayday meeting. "Perhaps you'll stop mooning about now," said Fred senior.

Time for one more reading, Norah told them. She had already read the cards for three of the ladies, and time was getting short; Norman was keen, until she produced the Death card, and even though she told him it didn't literally mean death, but that it signified transition and that he should put the past behind him, he was left speechless and a sickly white.

The clairvoyance evening got off to a good start, with Iris the postwoman convinced that her late cousin Cyril had tried to make contact – after all, no-one else in the room had a connection with anyone called Cyril, although Norah at first was querying whether anyone had ever had a pet squirrel.

Someone else at the back of the room started crying with joy at the thought that the dark-haired woman trying to make a connection was her great grandmother, despite her great grandmother having had a lovely head of snowy white hair.

Then Norah went quiet for a couple of minutes before she said: "There is someone here, but they are from a long, long time ago, and

I sense that it is a man who suffered a violent and painful death. It is a soldier."

There were anxious glances exchanged around the room, because a number of the people present had lost loved ones in war. "I hope it's great uncle Bert who died on D-Day," Dennis whispered to Joe sitting next to him.

"Shhh, he's coming through now, he's a Roman soldier called Titus, and I get the impression he has already made some sort of contact with someone in this room, someone he met in this village, but I can't work out what he means," said Norah.

What little colour there was in Norman's face now drained completely, as he thought back to the night on the seawall when he, Sid and Joe had gone ghost hunting, and he and Sid believed they had seen the ghost of a Roman soldier from the fort that once stood there.

"Has he mentioned any names?" asked Norman, visibly shaken. "No names, I think he just wants to let someone know that he is here," said Norah.

Norman sat back in his chair, taking stock of what had just happened, before disappearing downstairs to the bar. "It's been a funny old business up there, Peggy love, I don't know quite what to think. I don't know whether it's true, or just coincidence, but it's certainly a rum do. Oh, and I'd better have another pint and a bag of scratchings, Peggy love."

Upstairs, the evening had finished on a high note, with everyone happy with what they had seen and heard, especially Dennis, deep in conversation with Norah.

"It was very unprofessional of me to make something up like that, Dennis, but you've been such a good friend to my boy Charles, who I wish you wouldn't insist on calling Nozzer, I've made an exception just this once."

Chapter 18

History Bites Back

"Come now, ladies, I have important information to impart, and it affects every one of us," Mrs Gladman announced to the assembled gossips and tittle-tattlers who make up the inner sanctum of Little Bardon Women's Institute.

"This is such an important topic that I know you ladies of the committee will want to be told before I announce it to Tuesday's meeting."

Mrs Barnes and Mrs Ferguson, who rank very highly in the village gossiping league, were desperate to hear more - to hear something that they could each turn into a skilfully embroidered story to pass on, in strictest confidence, of course.

The two ladies were fairly fizzing with excitement, when self-important Mrs Gladman confided: "What I have to tell you is simply wonderful news. We, Little Bardon Women's Institute, have been chosen to lead a ground-breaking project that I know you will all be as excited about as I am."

"Yes, well tell us what it is, then, don't keep us guessing," said an impatient Mrs Ferguson.

"Of course, of course," replied a flustered Mrs Gladman. "We have been chosen by the parish council to produce a history of Little Bardon, and of the people who have lived here in this marvellous community over the course of history. I am personally very honoured that Major

Dobson, who as you all know is the esteemed chairman of the parish council, has asked me to lead the project.

"I am confident, and it is confidence shared by Major Dobson, that such a project will feature on local radio and probably on regional television. I am so excited." "Is that it?" asked Mrs Barnes. "We thought it would be something important, like getting a proper bus service at last. Now that would really be something to crow about."

The committee meeting descended into something akin to chaos, with one or two of the ladies genuinely excited at the prospect of delving into the past, but others, like Mrs Ferguson, Mrs Barnes and Miss Smith, more interested in what biscuits were in the tin marked 'WI use only'.

When Mrs Gladman presented her exciting news to Tuesday's WI meeting, there was what could best be described as a muted response.

"Oh, come, come, ladies, please show a little enthusiasm. Major Dobson has specifically asked that I, errh we, should lead this project, so we need to start planning how the tasks should be allocated," Mrs Gladman told the ladies, whose lack of enthusiasm was noticeable.

"I bet old Major Miseryguts won't do any of Mrs Gladman's tasks, but he'll want any glory that's going," whispered Mrs Barnes to Miss Smith and Mrs Ferguson.

"And what about yourself, Mrs Gladman, have you allocated a task to yourself?" asked Mrs Ferguson. "I shall co-ordinate, and collate the information that you ladies gather," was the reply.

"Perhaps it would be better if I were the co-ordinator," interjected super-haughty Mrs Nixon-Smith. "I was involved in something of a similar nature, although much larger, of course, when I lived in Surbiton."

"I think not, Mrs Nixon-Smith, I have your name against a most important task, to interview our elderly residents to glean their memories of the days when the village had bucket toilets, and weekly collections by what were termed, I believe, the night-soil men," responded Mrs Gladman, with the hint of a smile.

Mrs Gladman produced her familiar clipboard and reeled off the tasks she had thoughtfully allocated. Mrs Gill was less than enthusiastic about compiling a history of the post office, where she worked, and Miss Smith thought it of little value to look at the history of the council houses, built in the late 1920s, where she had lived for all of her adult life.

As well as memories, Mrs Gladman told the ladies that Major Dobson had emphasised the importance of photographs, then went into a long reminisce about the day she and her late husband moved to the village – where her great grandparents had spent all their lives – 43 years before, directly after their marriage.

Despite a certain amount of reticence on the part of some of the WI ladies, the majority soon got into the swing of digging out village history – quite simply because it meant they could be nosey officially.

There were one or two hiccoughs along the way, such as Miss Smith being given short shrift when she questioned farmer Reggie Naylor about rumours concerning his father and a young Land Army girl sent to help on the farm during the war.

"It was just silly talk," said a disgruntled Reggie, "and anyway, my dad was a very young man then, and it was long before he met my mother, and the baby could have been anybody's."

Mrs Cotton was similarly miffed when Mrs Gill questioned her about the night, 20 years before, when her tumbledown livery stables burned down in what the police said at the time was definitely an arson attack. "It happened, and that's all I'll say, and if I hear anything again about insurance fraud, I'll sue." Said Mrs Cotton, who is grumpy and argumentative even on one of her better days.

Fascinating facts started to emerge from the ladies' research, such as about who had the first wireless set in Little Bardon and who laid claim to having the first television, about the start of the bus service to Malbury, the old village pump and about some of the old characters who lived and worked there.

Characters like Elias Haysack, in the 1920s and 30s, who swept the chimneys in every village and farmstead for five or six miles around, going out every morning in his pony and trap, and often relying on the pony to trot home under his own steam while Elias slept in the trap after a detour to one of the pubs along the way.

Memories of the King's Head produced some fascinating facts, such as the Rat and Sparrow Club, beyond living memory, when a penny was paid for every rat and squirrel tail produced, and a bounty was paid on dead sparrows.

The recollection of a table skittles league at the pub stirred Norman, a leading light in today's darts team, to want to know more. "That would be a great winter game," he told Mrs Ferguson, who was gathering the information.

Mrs Gladman became more excited about the progress of the project each time the ladies got together to share their findings. "Major Dobson is going to be so impressed. He is already talking about a permanent exhibition of our history in the village hall," said a beaming Mrs Gladman. "But don't forget, ladies, that we need our elderly residents to dig out their old photographs."

Mrs Gladman would come to regret those words when the hunt for photographs really got under way.

Mrs Gill borrowed two albums from Mr Barrett who lived at the old people's bungalows, which chronicled village life, often in a somewhat blurry way, for a little more than three decades; there were events and people and generally feel-good photographs of villagers enjoying themselves on the green and in the street.

Mrs Ferguson also produced a whole stash of black and white photographs which elderly Mrs Lewis had hidden away under her bed.

"Right, let's have a look at these, spread them out on the table, come on ladies, chop chop," said Mrs Gladman, keen to peruse a little more village history. "But excuse me first, ladies, nature calls."

"Ooh, look, there's Mavis who I was at school with, and her brother Peter, playing on the green," said Mrs Barnes, "and there's my auntie Hilda. But who's that couple cuddled up on the grass, in the background, under the tree?"

"Let me look," said Mrs Ferguson. "That looks like, no it can't be."

"Let me have a look as well," said Miss Smith. "Yes, I'm sure it's her, but the young man is in soldier's uniform, and her husband was never in the forces. Oh dear, put it away quickly, before she comes back from the ladies."

Mrs Gladman returned with a huge smile. "Is there anything of great note in the photographs, ladies?"

"No, nothing really exciting," said Miss Smith as she slipped the offending photograph into her handbag, and exchanged her own huge smile with Mrs Ferguson and Mrs Barnes.

"We can all learn so much from old photographs, don't you agree, ladies; what's the photograph you've got there, Miss Smith?" said Mrs Gladman to a sea of beaming faces.

Chapter 19

The Tin Man

"Get those out of the bar, I won't keep telling you, you can't run your cheapjack business from this pub, Charlie's already warned you."

And indeed, landlord Charlie had told Billy numerous times to stop selling dubious items in the King's Head, but Billy didn't listen.

"Go on, get that old sack out of the bar. I don't know what's in it, but I'm pretty sure some of it is those dented tins of food that some people are mug enough to buy," said barmaid Peggy, pointing towards the door.

The dented tins, without labels, came from the canning factory just outside Malbury, and someone who Billy described as his 'secret contact' kept him supplied.

The trouble was that there was no way of knowing what was in any of the unlabeled tins, which was why Billy was often seen in the street pulling tins out of a hessian sack and handing them to someone who would shake each tin in turn to try to work out what was inside.

There was nothing illegal, because the tins were simply rejects because of dents and hadn't been stolen, but anyone dealing with Billy was taking a chance on whether their purchase was worth it or not; for some, the opportunity to buy a tin of something for a few pence, whether they really wanted the mystery contents or not, was too good to miss.

Billy mooched around the village, in gumboots, flat cap pulled over his eyes, tattered overcoat held together with a length of string, and trousers desperately needing a clean to get the mud off, looking like a down and out, but the truth was far different.

He owned a very desirable Victorian villa on the edge of the village, with a large garden, outbuildings and a paddock big enough to keep ponies if he had any.

What he did have was Jasper, his little Jack Russell terrier, and Monty the talking mynah bird, whose repertoire included several swearwords, although Billy was adamant that such language had only been learned off elderly chapel-goer Mrs Johns, who had been his 'daily' for years.

His garden was also home to a chicken run full of an assortment of fowls of various sizes and colours, and some rabbit hutches, always with an assortment of rabbits which eventually ended up as meals for whoever he could sell them to.

Far from needing to sell dented tins of food to make a little cash, he had more money than he would ever spend, from an inheritance rumoured to have been more than a million pounds, when he was 21, and that was nearly 60 years ago.

"Why don't you retire and put your feet up, instead of hawking these old tins around?" asked Peggy. "You could go somewhere warm and enjoy yourself."

"Enjoy myself! Don't talk daft, how would I enjoy myself, I don't like hot weather and I don't like foreign grub. Only a woman would say something like that. Anyway, I'd better have another pint before I go, Peggy love."

Dented tins were only a part of Billy's business empire; he could also supply sacks of horse manure to help village vegetable patches and allotments grow, and it was horse manure that almost got him arrested one evening.

It had been dark and raining, and Billy had just put the sack down beside him when he stopped to light one of his familiar roll-ups, when Pc Nicholls pulled up in his police car and asked: "What's in the sack?" to which Billy smiled and replied: "Horse muck."

"Don't be smart," said the young policeman, as he undid the string tying it up, then thrust his hand into the sack. "Oh, what!" he said as he pulled his hand out." This is, this is..."

"I know what it is, I told you what it is, but you told me I was being smart."

"I could nick you for this, but I'll let you off with a warning, and no, thank you, I don't want any for my garden, I'll make do with the bags of compost I get from the garden centre in Malbury. Now get on your way, before I change my mind."

Billy retold that story at every opportunity, just as he did his wartime tale of when he reckoned he was Winston Churchill's personal homing pigeon handler.

According to Billy, he and Churchill waited patiently in the War Department pigeon loft for a message-carrying pigeon to arrive from France. When it eventually flew in, he handed the message which had been attached to the pigeon's leg to Churchill, who picked up a phone and said "D-Day is on, D-Day is on."

No-one was ever convinced that Winston Churchill would have been standing, phone at the ready, in a mucky pigeon loft with Billy, waiting for a pigeon, but it was a story that earned Billy a few pints over the years from visitors intrigued to be meeting a true village character.

Then there was the day he met the Tiller Girls, and the day he went to Wales to collect a load of black-faced sheep from the top of a mountain which had become white-faced when they reached the bottom because of the exertion of being chased at full-tilt by a sheepdog.

And, of course, there were stories of black market activities during the war; according to Billy, he had dealt in just about everything the

Army possessed that was movable, although he said he drew the line at weapons. "Wouldn't have done to be caught with a gun or ammunition," he told his audience, "although if you could eat it, drink it or wear it, I could get it."

There were even more outrageous tales, which became more extreme at each telling, and most of the regulars in the King's Head had heard them over and over again. Billy was indeed a character, but sadly one of a dying breed.

Other characters in the village over the years had included Billy's friend Alfred, who somehow scraped a living looking after ponies for people. He was very partial to jugged hare, and visitors to his back door frequently had to brush their way past a dead hare which had been hanging on a nail for two or three weeks; he wouldn't dream of eating one that had been dead for less than a fortnight.

Billy had never married, and had never sought out female company, unless they were visitors gullible enough to stand in the pub open-mouthed at his stories, and willing to refill his glass when he made a point of saying how much he had enjoyed his pint, but it would have to be his last as his money must have fallen through the hole in his trouser pocket.

Peggy always gave him one of her icy stares when he came out with that well-worn line, but so long as the visitor was happy to buy the beer and to listen to another tall tale, she figured it wasn't for her to complain.

Then came the day that Peggy bumped into Mrs Johns in the bakery and mentioned that she hadn't seen Billy in the pub for a few days.

"Haven't you heard?" asked Mrs Johns, "He fell down the stairs on Sunday night, hit his head and sadly died. The policeman told me it looked as if he tripped over a sack of tins on the landing."

Chapter 20

The Last Cowboy

The weekly pension queue at the post office is probably the most depressing place to be in Little Bardon, and the misery seems to get worse each time its elderly patrons meet outside to moan and groan, and then continue inside in true misery.

Mrs Gatehouse always complains about her bunions and about how the NHS doesn't care about people who have worked hard all their lives, although that argument immediately falls flat as she has never worked since she married almost 60 years ago.

Mrs Darby suffers in a whisper with piles and says the NHS is a wonderful service, which always ensures an argument with Mrs Gatehouse, and Mr Barrett always livens up the pension queue with his noisy flatulence.

Then there is old Garth, who announces his arrival with a jangling of spurs and a friendly "howdy"; always looking rather magnificent in stetson and fringed suede jacket, Garth is the village's last cowboy – in fact, and it must be said to set the record straight, the village's only cowboy.

Now in his late seventies, he became obsessed with cowboys from the first black and white western film he saw at the old Gaumont cinema in Malbury. After that, life was never the same; John Wayne, Robert Mitchum and a host of Hollywood stars became Garth's heroes.

The customers on his milk round became used to being addressed as 'pardner' and 'good buddy', although some elderly ladies had been a little disconcerted when Garth started wearing a gunbelt, albeit with fake guns, but that was quickly declared a no-no by his bosses at the dairy.

He loved living his version of the cowboy lifestyle, but without the horse because, although he was loathe to admit it, he was scared of the big, smelly creatures, and even more scared of what his wife Doris would say if he brought one home.

There also wouldn't be room in his council house garden for anything other than his rickety old shed, his chickens and Doris' vegetable patch, and Doris was adamant anyway that no large animal would be allowed anywhere near her neatly tended plot.

She always contended that Gordon – which was his real name before he decided that Garth had a better cowboy sound to it – was a complete crackpot whose delusions she could live with but were best ignored whenever possible.

They have seldom gone out together because Doris refuses to walk with a man in a stetson, fringed suede jacket, cowboy boots and spurs, and anyway, she asked him, how many other cowboys walk with a stick.

It has always hurt a little that Doris won't take his arm for a Sunday afternoon stroll along the village street, but hurts even more that his son Terry has no interest in cowboys, and anyway thinks his father's obsession with the wild west, while mostly harmless, is bizarre.

"Can't you take up a hobby like fishing or bowls or something, dad? People round here think you're crackers. Don't you think you're a bit old now to pretend you're Roy Rogers?" Terry said to him one day.

"Pretend, what do you mean pretend?" and with that, disgruntled Garth went down the garden to the shed where he spent most of his time, and where even Doris was not allowed inside. "You've got your kitchen, I've got my shed," he told her.

Doris had told him long ago that she would not dress as either a cowgirl or a squaw, and she said no self-respecting Little Bardon woman would dress as a Dodge City saloon girl, despite Garth telling her repeatedly that it was just harmless fun "and then I'd let you come into the shed."

She was happy for the shed to be his sole domain, and had no wish to venture inside. She was amused when he hung up a sign saying 'Ponderosa', the ranch home of his heroes of many years ago, TV's Cartwright family of 'Bonanza' fame, and smiled every time she went down the garden and heard the scratchy strains of a theme tune from a western film coming from Garth's elderly record player.

Other men have train sets in their sheds to live out their fantasies, and Garth has got whatever he needs to live out his own fantasy of being a cowboy, she figured, so if it keeps him happy let him get on with it.

She often wondered what was in the shed that took up so much of Garth's time, and why he always came out of it with a big beaming smile, but the padlock on the door and grubby net curtain at the little window thwarted unwanted attention.

It must be something to do with that huge piece of wood that Young Fred and his dad Fred senior brought round in a truck and carried, with some difficulty, into the shed, she reasoned.

As time went by, Doris' curiosity grew beyond wondering what the wood was for, why she occasionally heard the sound of chiselling, and why Garth sometimes appeared with bright paint splashes on him.

"No, Doris, I can't tell you, it's a surprise," he repeatedly told her as he disappeared back into his shed, carefully closing the door behind him. "You'll know soon enough."

One evening, curiosity got the better of her and she crept down the garden with a torch, while Garth snoozed in front of the TV; she had barely shone it through the net curtain when a voice behind her said: "You can't wait, can you, you just can't wait. You just want to spoil my surprise. You've upset me now."

Doris was mortified that her beloved Garth might really be angry with her. "I just want to know what you're doing in your shed," said Doris. "You mean in the 'Ponderosa'," said Garth with an adopted American twang, cowboy style. "You will know next week, and you'll see what I've been working hard on, especially for your birthday. It's something you told me you've always wanted."

Doris scratched her head, trying to think of anything she had told him she had always wanted, but the only thing she could think of was telling Garth she had always wanted a stainless steel bowl, for mixing cakes, like they have at the doctor's, what the surgery receptionist told her was called, for some unknown reason, a lotion bowl, but he would hardly be making one of those in his shed.

Over the next few days, Garth spent every waking hour working on the mystery that he was planning to surprise Doris with. Then, on the next Sunday, the two Freds arrived to move it out of the shed.

"Don't get any lighter, does it Garth. Blimey, you've done a good job on it, looks real professional," said Fred senior as he puffed and panted. "I didn't expect it to look as good as this."

"This is brilliant," said Young Fred. "Do you reckon you can make me one?"

When they got to the front garden, Garth's son Terry drove up, and got out of his car, visibly shocked. "I don't know quite what to say, dad, I didn't expect anything like this," said Terry in disbelief.

Doris just stood open-mouthed, and turned to Terry: "I told him I had always wanted a lotion bowl, but the silly old sod just doesn't listen."

You will always know Garth's house if you drive along Little Bardon's village street – it's the only one with a ten feet tall, carved and painted totem pole in the front garden.

"Well, what do you think? Is it as nice as you expected? Happy birthday," said Garth.

"It's perfect, just what I have always wanted."

Chapter 21

Fitness Fiasco

It was unusually solemn in the public bar of the King's Head on what was usually a happy and jovial Friday evening; there were long faces and a definite slowing down of the normal drinking rate. It was obvious that something was amiss in sleepy Little Bardon.

"What's the problem tonight, boys? You lot are usually gobby, but not tonight," said Peggy behind the bar. "Something is bothering you all. Come on, tell auntie Peggy."

"Truth is, Peggy love, there's a conspiracy against us," said a doleful-looking Dennis. "Our wives have ganged up on us and decided we all need to lose weight and get fit.

"You won't believe this, but I had salad for me tea tonight. I got back from the allotment expecting a nice fry up, but no, she says, it's salad or nothing. And then she had the cheek to call me Mr Fatso."

There were nods of condolence from along the bar as others declared that they too had been given a get-fit-or-else ultimatum. Sid, Joe, Norman and Fred senior admitted that they were under strict orders to get fit and trim. "And me," shouted Conrad with the tricky eye from his familiar spot at the fruit machine. "My wife Pearl says I've got to lose my gut. The cheek of it."

Young Fred arrived with his mates Mark and Jason, and immediately started barracking his father, laughing about how long he would survive on lettuce leaves and radishes. "You'll laugh on the other side of your face when you get home," said Fred senior. "Your mum says you need to lose a bit of weight as well, so you'll be joining me on the rabbit food."

"Does this mean you'll be cutting out beer and pork scratchings?" asked Peggy, an acknowledged tester of countless diets, her latest involving large quantities of mushrooms and glasses of cold cabbage water.

"No, no, Peggy love, beer is good for you, and scratchings are only a bit of pig skin so they can't be fattening. But I've told my missus I'll give up eating crisps," retorted Norman, genuinely hurt that anyone would dream of suggesting giving up his nightly pints of Old Todger and bags of scratchings.

"Thank Heaven for that, I thought I might be out of a job," laughed Peggy. "So how are you going to do this, then? Are you planning to start exercising other than lifting pints?"

"What we thought was, having our healthy stuff at home, then down here in the evenings for a few pints as usual. And if you could get some pies in, steak and kidney, chicken, that sort of thing, and maybe some nice cakes, we could all top up on decent grub when we're here, secretive like," said Dennis.

Then came the big question. "What about the exercise? Won't your other halves expect you to make just a little bit of effort on that score?" asked Peggy.

Walking to the pub was the only exercise one or two of them got, and the thought of joining a gym or investing in a bike was a definite no-no.

Then Young Fred suggested: "Why don't we have an exercise class on the village green on a Sunday morning? Everyone will see then that we're making a real effort, and it won't cost us anything, and we can come back here for a lunchtime session."

Brilliant suggestion, Young Fred, they all agreed, but who would run the class? "Let's ask Iris the postwoman," said Sid. "She's no spring chicken, but she must be fit because she's out delivering on her bike every day. I'll ask her. Will you be joining us, Peggy love? Might be good to lose a few pounds." Peggy's reaction is unrecorded, but suffice to say that Sid made a hasty exit from the pub.

Iris thought it a wonderful idea when Sid bumped into her a few days later and told her that she had topped the shortlist of possible instructors, particularly because it was obviously her own supreme fitness that had ensured her ageless looks and girlish figure.

"I'm flattered that you have asked me; of course I'll help you all get fit. But there will be no slacking out there. I can be a hard taskmaster."

The following Saturday was Norman's birthday, so the evening drinking session was even more boozy than a normal Saturday night, ending with birthday boy Norman being unceremoniously dumped in the pub garden's ornamental pond.

Sunday morning on the village green was like a scene from a zombie movie. To their credit, Sid, Dennis and the two Freds were there dead on ten, but, in truth, all four looked more dead than alive.

The only one who looked even slightly athletic was Young Fred, in fetching red shorts and multi-coloured t-shirt, but looks can be very deceptive, as the others agreed when he was violently ill over the memorial bench and had to take his shirt off to clean it up.

"Is this it, then? Just the four of you?" asked a disappointed Iris, who was resplendent in her granddaughter's pink tracksuit, stretched to bursting point, and dayglo headband.

"We'll start with a slow jog around the green to get loosened up. Ah, here come some others. Come on, come on, join in." Joe and Norman did their best to jog, but it was beyond the abilities of a pair of living corpses to do anything but walk.

A couple of wives stood laughing on the edge of the green as their husbands struggled to perform even the most basic exercises, and Pc Nicholls got out of his patrol car to stand watching, shaking his head in disbelief, particularly at the sight of Norman sinking to his knees on the grass, gasping for breath.

Iris had spent the last couple of evenings watching YouTube exercise videos, so felt she was now a competent trainer, and was ready to knock this rough bunch into shape, which is exactly what she had told Mrs Barnes when she bumped into her en route to church.

"Right, jump up and down on the spot, and clap your hands in the air. Put your water bottle down first, Dennis, or at least put the lid on, to stop it splashing everywhere, and Norman, get off the grass now and put some effort in," said Iris, displaying the enthusiasm of a woman possessed.

"Now I think we will do some press ups. Will someone help Norman off his knees, and Young Fred, stop complaining about your throbbing head."

There were hilarious attempts at squat thrusts that ended in total chaos as both Fred senior and Joe lay on the grass complaining about knee pain and Norman said he thought he was about to have a heart attack.

Iris accused Young Fred and Joe of being too lazy to exercise properly, and declared that she thought she was wasting her time trying to get them fit.

Disgruntled Iris was just about to go home when Conrad with the tricky eye came bounding across the village green, dressed in a smart new tracksuit, followed by his rather large wife Pearl in matching kit.

"I told you I'd get him here, Iris, and I have, and I've decided that we are both going to get fit, ready for a walking holiday in the Peak District."

Iris had Conrad and Pearl running, jumping and generally waggling arms, legs and heads in time to the crackly CD player she had brought with her, watched from their prone positions on the grass by Sid, Dennis, Joe, Norman and the two Freds, and from the road by Pc Nicholls, who was enjoying enormously the Sunday morning spectacle.

Then disaster struck, as Iris clutched the small of her back, Conrad twisted his ankle, Pearl collapsed in a heavy-breathing heap and the six on the grass were all struggling to get to their feet, and complaining about pulling muscles none of them really knew if they actually had.

"I think that's enough for this morning, Iris. Thank you for your expert help," said Sid, fighting for breath as he tried to stand.

Young Fred had made it to his feet and done the gentlemanly thing and helped Iris up, still clutching her back, but forcing a smile as she told them: "Any time I can help, lads, you know you've just got to ask."

What followed was like the aftermath of a battle, with the wounded staggering off to find any help they could. For Iris it was round to Mrs Barnes' for a cup of tea and the chance to rub some linament into her back, and for the rest a much-needed stagger to the King's Head.

"People usually look like you lot when they're leaving, not when they're coming in to the pub," said Peggy, as she instinctively moved to the Old Todger hand pump to start pulling the much-needed pints.

"Do I take it that your exercise class was harder than you expected?"

"No, I think we all came through it pretty well," said Dennis, as Peggy went off to answer the pub phone.

She returned with a glum look on her face. "That was Mrs Barnes. She said to tell you lot that Iris is on her way to hospital for an x-ray. She reckons she's pulled something nasty in her back."

Chapter 22

Carnival Day

Margaret had lived in Little Bardon for all of her 84 years; she had married at St Stephen's, brought up three sons to be fine men and generally had a good life, loved by the community of which she had always been such an integral part.

But now she knew there was not very much more of that life left; her health had been failing, her dependence on medication and a constant hook-up to oxygen becoming more acute.

But her fierce independence meant she still lived alone in her little bungalow, bed-ridden, but with the support of two of her daughters-in-law who lived nearby, and with the help of community nurses and carers.

She lived surrounded by happy memories, with framed family photographs full of smiles and laughter, and with the biggest smile on the face of a young woman on a carnival float – the black and white photograph was of 20-year-old Margaret when she was Malbury's carnival queen all those years ago, something she described as one of the happiest days of her life.

"Is that really you?" one of the nurses asked her one day. "You were a beautiful young woman, Margaret. You must have been so excited to be chosen as carnival queen."

"It was a wonderful day. I think about it a lot now, and just wish I could live it all over again, but that can't ever happen, can it. I never imagined, on that wonderful carnival day all those years ago, that this is how I would end up."

She said that with a smile - there was no self-pity, no resentment, it was just a matter-of-fact statement about how things were.

Meanwhile, the village was planning its first carnival for three years, just the usual small event, with fun and games on the village green and a procession along the village street, with a few floats and, of course, the carnival queen.

"We'll make sure we get you outside to watch the procession, then perhaps one of your daughters-in-law can wheel you along to the village green," said nurse Jackie. "Might even manage an ice cream and some candy floss, eh, Margaret."

Margaret gave one of her biggest smiles, but there was a look of sadness in her eyes, and Jackie knew exactly what she must do.

Her next visit that day was to Miss Smith, who was on the carnival committee, followed by a phone call to Margaret's daughter-in-law Iris the postwoman, who told her: "It's a wonderful idea, let's do it."

And so the plans started to be laid, with the help of the committee, to make carnival day one that Margaret would never forget, a day that would make a dream come true for this kind, gentle woman.

"Mum, you're going to have a lovely day, watching the carnival procession and then enjoying a fun afternoon," Iris told her, all the while fearful that it might be too much for the frail woman's health.

A consultation with the community nurses and carers helped Iris and the family decide how much they could safely expect Margaret to manage on the day.

"We can borrow a wheelchair so we can push you outside to watch, then go along to the village green and spend some of the afternoon there," Iris told her.

The day couldn't come along quickly enough for Margaret; every day she daydreamed about what it would be like to go outside for the first time in nearly a year, to breathe fresh air again and feel the sun on her face.

But her thoughts always ended on a sad note, thinking back to her day as carnival queen all those years ago, the wonderful day when she beamed and waved to those happy faces lining Malbury's streets, but a wonderful day that could never be repeated, a day that had to stay locked away as a memory.

Sadly, her health continued to deteriorate, and a question mark hung over whether Margaret would be well enough to enjoy carnival day, but she told nurse Jackie a few days before: "You just try stopping me, I'm going to get outside and enjoy myself if it's the last thing I do."

Carnival day started with nurse and carer visits, and then it seemed as if the whole world was coming through her front door. First one son and wife, then a second and a third, together with four grandchildren and Mrs Grimmer from next door, who brought Margaret a bunch of flowers to add to the three bunches from daughters-in-law.

"I feel just like a queen, this is so lovely," Margaret told them all. "This is going to be such a special day."

She was overwhelmed by all the familiar faces she saw and by the number of old friends who came up and told her how lovely it was to see her again, as son Tony pushed her slowly to the village green, where activities were already getting underway.

"This is beautiful, just beautiful," she said, with a tear in her eye, as Tony pushed her past the nine colourful floats being prepared for the procession, and past Malbury Majorettes practising their twirls and fancy steps.

Danford Boys Brigade Band were warming up and pride-filled mothers of village children in fancy dress were making last minute adjustments to costumes.

"Some of them look a bit scary," said Margaret, pointing to Spiderman and a ten-year-old dressed as a zombie. "They're going to have such a wonderful experience. I feel quite jealous.

"Where are we going to be to watch the parade? I am going to get a good view, I hope. This might be the last one I see."

"You're going to have the best seat of the day, mum, we've all made sure of that," said Tony, as he pushed her towards farmer Reggie Naylor, standing with his Shire horses Major and Tommy, harnessed to a beautifully restored farm waggon.

"All ready now," said Reggie, "The rugby club lads will provide the muscle we need," and with that four burly rugby players lifted the wheelchair on to the back of the waggon and strapped it down.

A colourful blanket was wrapped around Margaret, her bunches of flowers were put into her lap, and Reggie urged his two beautiful horses into motion, brasses gleaming, harness shining and Margaret with the widest smile as they moved sedately off to lead the procession through the village.

"Now who says dreams don't come true," said Margaret to herself as she wiped away a tear; the heavy farm waggon, resplendent in shiny blue and red paint, lumbered slowly along the village street behind Major and Tommy, with Reggie Naylor at the reins and his son Jim walking at the horses' heads.

What a sight we are, thought Margaret as she acknowledged the waves of villagers who shouted and called to her, and some threw the flowers they had bought after the plans for Margaret's special day became the village's worst kept secret earlier in the week.

Margaret's mind was becoming a blur as the procession moved slowly along the street; she saw the faces of her friends in the crowds, and then her parents were there, cheering her on, on that wonderful day in Malbury so many years before.

And there was her sister Rosemary who had died before her twenty first birthday, and her little dog Timmy who had been her companion all those years ago.

Her grandmother was smiling at five-year-old Margaret running around her garden. Her grandfather waved from his vegetable plot at the end of the garden, and there were her schoolfriends in their summer dresses, playing around the pond, running away from that nasty boy Richard who pulled the legs off frogs.

It was all there in front of her, all of those wonderful things in her life, and then her eyes gently closed and very, very slowly it faded and was gone.

Chapter 23

Sorry, Auntie Gladys

"Careful, Young Fred, careful, you'll knock me off this bar stool before I've even managed to get on it."

"Sorry, Auntie Gladys, but don't you think you'd be better in a comfy chair round in the saloon bar?"

Auntie Gladys said no, definitely not. She wanted to see where her favourite great nephew spent his evenings, and anyway, it was darts night, and she loved darts.

"Good evening, welcome to the King's Head. You must be Young Fred's Auntie Gladys who we've been hearing so much about. Now, can I get you both a drink? I know it'll be a pint of Old Todger and a bag of scratchings for you, Young Fred, but what about you, Gladys?"

"Do you want a sherry or something, auntie?" asked Young Fred. "No, I'll have whatever you're drinking," was the surprise answer.

"Make that two pints then, Peggy love, and do you want anything to eat, auntie, scratchings, crisps, a couple of pickled eggs?"

Peggy slid the pints across the bar, and whispered: "Young Fred, you really know how to treat a lady, don't you, offering your dear old auntie pickled eggs. How old is she, by the way?" Auntie Gladys confided that she was approaching her eighty fourth birthday, and usually drank pints of Guinness, "but I can't handle it now like I used to. Four pints now and I feel a bit unsteady on my feet. And I will have a couple of pickled eggs, it's a long time since I got my gums round a nice pickled egg, but just a word of warning, they can play havoc with my innards."

"Four pints over here, please, Peggy love, and four bags of scratchings." The order came from Dennis, newly arrived with Joe, Sid and Fred senior. "This must be Auntie Gladys, who we've been hearing about."

Fred senior gave his auntie a hug and asked: "Did Young Fred organise a taxi for you from Malbury?" "No, I came on the back of his motorbike," she said. "It was a bit breezy. My skirt kept blowing up, but it was fun."

"It would have been more fun if you'd listened to what I told you about leaning with the bike," said Young Fred, watching Auntie Gladys drain her first pint.

She quickly became the centre of attention, getting her lips round her second pint and scoffing a second bag of scratchings. Peggy was a little worried that she could end up with a medical emergency on her hands, but Fred senior assured her that Auntie Gladys was as tough as nails and in her younger days could have out-drunk anyone in the bar.

Peggy looked up, and saw Sid coming back from the gents. "Do you have to do that? Do you have to sniff your fingers when you come out of the gents? You'll put customers off."

"Sorry, Peggy love, but I like the smell of the new soap in the dispenser," said Sid.

"That's what you say. You sure they haven't run out of paper," said Dennis, as he pushed another pint in front of Auntie Gladys.

"Time we got the arrers out, boys. I'm feeling lucky tonight," said Fred senior, whose skill at darts was only slightly more impressive than his tuneless singing.

"There were shouts of "Shut it" and "Not now" as he broke into 'The Wild Rover', and thankfully he took his friends' advice, but he was always ready for a burst of dreadful singing whenever the opportunity arose.

"I used to love singing 'The Wild Rover', so perhaps we could sing it together later on, Fred," said Auntie Gladys who, by now, was starting to look slightly the worse for wear. "Those pickled eggs were nice, so I think I'll try another couple, and a bag of scratchings that the boys seem to enjoy so much," she told Peggy, who asked her: "How are you enjoying your Old Todger. You'll soon be needing a refill, from the looks of it."

Auntie Gladys agreed that a fourth pint would be very acceptable, so Young Fred topped her up with beer, pickled eggs, scratchings and the two bags of cheese and onion crisps which she said she fancied.

"You don't see many little old ladies knocking back pints and eating the mixture she's getting through. I just hope she don't burst," laughed Peggy to Dennis. "She's certainly some character."

Even the most hardened of the hardened drinkers spread along the bar were in awe of Auntie Gladys' capacity for beer and pub snacks, as a fifth pint appeared, and quickly disappeared, and yet more pickled eggs, crisps and scratchings were consumed.

"Where the heck's she putting it all?" Sid whispered to Young Fred. "It's not natural." And nor were the rasping sounds that emanated from Auntie Gladys' direction.

"Oops, sorry boys, was that me?" Auntie Gladys slurred, as everyone agreed that yes, it definitely was her. It was enough to make most of the crowd move back from the bar and towards the dart board, where Dennis beat Sid, Norman gave Joe a thrashing and Fred senior lost badly to Charlie the landlord.

"I don't believe this," said Peggy as she served up pint number six to glassy-eyed Gladys. "I'm getting really worried that she's going to fall off that bar stool," she told Fred senior. "Look after your auntie before she has an accident."

Fred senior did as he was bid, and stood close beside Gladys, with Young Fred providing a buffer on the other side, although the look he gave Peggy let her know he was regretting standing so close when the effects of pickled eggs numbers five and six started to become obvious.

"I've had a lovely evening, boys, and there's only one thing more I would like to do before you take me home, Young Fred, have a game of darts."

There were looks of alarm as the darts players contemplated this drunken old lady being let loose with a fistful of darts.

"Are you sure that's such a good idea, Gladys dear, you don't want to hurt yourself. Why don't you let me make you a nice cup of tea?" Peggy asked her.

No, Gladys was adamant that she was going to play darts, so was eased off the bar stool and helped to the oche, assuring Charlie that she would mind his lights and definitely wouldn't injure anyone.

Her assurances did nothing to encourage anyone to stand within hitting range, and there were some who thought it certain she wouldn't even be able to hit the board.

"Can you remember how to do it?" asked Fred senior, swaying unsteadily beside her. "Of course I do, you great lump, I was playing darts before you were born."

She stood, supported on her walking stick in her left hand, and with one eye closed, and let the first dart go.

One or two people instinctively flinched, but all were amazed when it hit a double 19, then the second dart thudded into a single 20 and the third scored a double top.

The whole bar went quiet, as people looked at each other, shaking their heads in amazement, then burst into cheers and applause.

"I've still got it," she mumbled almost incoherently to Fred senior, who told the bar: "I should have said, really, Auntie Gladys was county ladies darts champion 50 or so years ago, so I'm just glad she never tried to play anyone for money."

Chapter 24

Rumours

In a small village, an off-hand remark, a tiny morsel of misinformation, or some less than intelligent guesswork, quickly becomes highly-embellished fact.

In the hands of accomplished gossips Mrs Barnes, Mrs Ferguson and their friends, the smallest non-fact takes on encyclopaedic proportions as it moves through Little Bardon at lightning speed from mouth to mouth.

"You know me, I'm not one to gossip," Iris the postwoman tells everyone she meets on her round, as the current rumour in her capable hands spreads at supersonic speed.

There was a true transatlantic rumour back in the 1980s that US President George Bush was heading for Little Bardon in search of ancestors.

According to a newspaper, a man called Reynold Bush from Messing, a small village only a few dozen miles from Little Bardon, had sailed from Ipswich in 1631 and settled in Massachusetts. His descendants included the president, who was now trying to track down more family members.

That was enough to set Little Bardon's oldest inhabitant, Fred Glee, thinking back to his boyhood and to his dad telling him about Charlie Bush, the local thatcher, who died years before Fred was born. "I'll be damned if he weren't one of that old President's family, I'm certain sure of that," Fred told the eager ears of all and sundry and, before long, it became fact.

The village went into overdrive, preparing for the visit of a US President who, for security reasons, quite obviously would rely on a surprise visit, they reasoned. When the visit was spoken of by the legion of village gossips, it was in hushed tones for fear of being overheard by a foreign spy, although in a small village a foreigner would have stood out like the proverbial sore thumb.

Mrs Lampson, on instruction from her neighbours on either side, kept watch from her front window for the presidential motorcade for five days before she decided that he obviously wasn't coming.

That was followed by the devastating news from Fred Glee that his memory wasn't what it once was, and the thatcher was actually Butcher, Charlie Butcher. "Well, I'll be blowed, I could've sworn it were Bush. I think my memory must be going," he told his sister Doreen when she made her regular Monday visit to collect his washing and deliver his clean set of clothes.

"You silly old fool, your memory went years ago," she said. "Don't go telling folks things if you're not sure. When I met Mrs Notting in the post office last week she told me she was so excited about the visit she was having a job to sleep nights."

Then there was the time that the Beckhams were buying The Grange, a Georgian house on the edge of the village, after old Mrs Moncrieff died. And it was also a known fact, a definite, solid, indisputable fact, that Victoria Beckham was planning to open a fashion store in the village.

"This is really going to put us on the map," said Mrs Ferguson. "I've had that information from the very top. It's 100% accurate, just wait and see." The village did just that, it waited and waited, and saw nothing.

It was conceded afterwards that only an idiot would ever have considered that Little Bardon could become the hub of a fashion empire, but no-one liked to tell Mrs Ferguson that, although Mrs Barnes was tempted to after she and Mrs Ferguson exchanged heated words over whose responsibility it had been to order the teabags for the Mothers' Union meeting.

The village hotbeds of rumour are the monthly meetings of the WI, the nightly drinking sessions in the public bar of the King's Head and the weekly pension queue at the post office.

The pension queue is particularly fond of a new rumour, either big or small, and if it puts anyone in the village in a compromising position, then so much the better.

Newcomers the Larkin family, who had recently moved to one of the new houses in Mill Road, became the subject of speculation which turned into a rumour, because they had two expensive cars.

"Something not right there. He's got that big old Range Rover and she drives about in that flashy little sports car, but none of the two of them work," Mrs Gill told Mrs Barnes from her gossip station behind the post office counter. Mrs Barnes passed on that nugget to Mrs Ferguson who handed it over to Miss Smith, and by the end of the day the whole village was talking about shady goings-on in Mill Road.

Mr and Mrs Larkin carried on their happy, highly-paid lives working from home as web designer and financial advisor, completely oblivious to the excitement they had unwittingly created, although Mrs Larkin told her husband: "Some of them around here are a bit strange, and they're certainly stand-offish. The woman in the post office gave me a very weird look today, and hardly spoke."

Hardly speaking is something quite alien to the village's top level of gossipers and rumour-mongers, who all try to get both the first and the last word. Iris the postwoman, for instance, who invariably includes "You know me, I'm not one to gossip," in every conversation, usually manages a bout of laryngitis each year, which others, behind her back of course, put down to excessive gabbling.

When laryngitis strikes, Ben the relief postman steps in to ensure the mail gets delivered, but that is all he delivers. He always has a big smile, a few friendly words, but no gossip and not even the merest hint of a rumour.

"He's a nice young chap," Mrs Gill told Mrs Barnes, "but he's never got anything interesting to say, never got any news. It's not the same without Iris. I don't know what we'll do if she decides to retire."

Then came the day that Iris dreaded, her throat was so painful and so inflamed that she simply couldn't speak. She tried, but the best she could manage was a rasping sound similar to sawing wood and, calamity of all calamities, she had some news to share, not rumour or gossip, but news about Major Dobson, the parish council chairman, being arrested in Malbury for enjoying rather too much hospitality at the Feathers pub and then driving home.

She rang Mrs Barnes in great but painful excitement, and tried desperately to share the hottest news for years, but simply couldn't get Mrs Barnes to understand her, and the call ended with Mrs Barnes imploring: "Iris, is that you, is that you, I can't understand anything you are saying, can you speak up? Is that you, Iris, speak up, speak up."

There were similar frustrating non-conversations with Mrs Ferguson and Mrs Gill, who both were unsure whether they were in fact being called by a husky-voiced man and whether they should call the police.

Iris had this incredible news, the most important she had heard for such a long time, but no way of passing it on. Someone else would find out, and have the pleasure of sharing it around the village, and Iris would lose her position as unofficial village newshound.

It was too much to bear. She pulled the duvet over her head and had a little weep into her pillow. But she was determined that having no voice would not stop her, so dragged herself out of bed, had a gargle with salt water, wrapped herself in a warm coat and her neck in a scarf and ventured out of her house for the first time in several days.

I'M NOT ONE TO GOSSIP

Desperate to share the hottest news the village had heard in years, Iris went first to Mrs Gill at the post office, but Mrs Gill was at a hospital appointment; the next stop was Mrs Barnes' door, but there was no reply, so in sheer desperation she hammered on Mrs Davis' door, hoping against hope that she would be in and ready to receive the startling revelation that was building up in Iris' mind to be the news of the decade.

Mrs Davis opened the door, and before Iris could attempt a croaky word, said: "Iris, you'll never guess." Iris slowly shook her head as if acknowledging that no, she couldn't guess whatever it was.

"You won't believe this, old Dobson has been nicked for drunk driving. It's all round the village. Everyone's talking about it."

Iris was certain at that point that her day could not get any worse. But then it did…

"And you won't believe this either, Iris, that snotty-nosed Mrs Nixon-Smith, her from Glebe House, was in the car with old Dobson."

Iris wanted to know if that highly valuable nugget of information had been shared with the whole village as well, but the words simply wouldn't come out. Sadly, she knew she had to finally admit defeat, and it hurt; oh, how it hurt.

Chapter 25

Sisters, Sisters

They seemed to have been around forever; they knew everyone in the village, and everyone knew them, and everyone always had a kind word for the two sisters who went everywhere together.

Where Edith went, Emily went, with Edith always walking ahead and Emily a couple of paces behind. If ever there were two devoted, inseparable sisters, it was these two.

At 81, Edith was the elder by a year, and the proud possessor of a fine set of pearly white dentures, which she liked to take out and examine at every opportunity. Emily made do with a few black stumps, and the promise of shiny new teeth when she could pluck up enough courage to visit the dentist in Malbury.

For now, though, Emily was happy to simply admire Edith's newly fitted mouth furniture at every opportunity, and dream of the day that she would look as good as her big sister,

Neither of them had ever married, although it was rumoured that in their teens they had each had a child; they had lived together all their lives, without known family around them, but always with at least one cat, and with a succession of small mongrel dogs.

Their pets played an important part in their lives, and unfortunately they regarded neutering of any of their cats an unkind act and unnecessary expense, which is why they always seemed to be finding homes for kittens.

"You won't believe it," Young Fred told the public bar drinking crowd in the King's Head one night, "I went round to pull a few weeds out of their garden for them, and they had just discovered that Tabby had had kittens, and they were already several weeks old."

"How come, surely they must have known when they were born," said barmaid Peggy.

"No, they were born in the back of the sofa, apparently, and they didn't know they were there because they are both deaf as posts, and because they're both forgetful I don't think they even remembered they had a cat. Do you want a nice little kitten, Peggy love? Oh, and a pint and a bag of scratchings over here, please."

Edith and Emily had both worked well into their sixties in the kitchen at the Green Man hotel in Malbury, and moved back to their home village Little Bardon when they retired.

There were a number of tales about their years at the Green Man, including the time the hot-blooded Spanish chef baked Edith's shoes in the oven.

"How on earth did that happen?" Peggy asked Young Fred when he was telling the story in the pub. "Apparently she kept putting her outdoor shoes in the warm oven so they wouldn't be cold when she went home, and he kept telling her not to, and warned her what he would do."

Young Fred had always had a soft spot for the sisters, living just a few doors away since he was a little boy. He kept their small garden tidy as a favour, but was never keen to go inside their home. When Peggy asked him once why he wasn't keen he told her there was no special reason, but held his nose as he mouthed "Cats".

"Do you know," Emily told Edith one day, "I'm blowed if I don't go and see that old dentist. You look lovely in them teeth, and I want to look as good as you. But where are your teeth, you haven't got them in?"

Edith's realisation that she hadn't put her teeth in that morning set off an alarming chain of events, because she simply could not remember where she had put them.

The two searched their little cottage for over an hour, but there was no sign of the errant teeth. "You haven't flushed them down the loo, have you, sister?" asked Emily. "When did you last have them in? You must have had them last night because you were eating an apple."

Edith simply couldn't remember, and started to become emotional at the thought that her lovely set of dentures might be gone forever. "If anyone comes to the door, you go, I can't let anyone see me like this," said Edith, but Emily reminded her that no-one ever came to the door, so that issue would not arise.

"I know, I know," Edith said in an excited voice. "I took them out when I was in the garden last night looking for Tabby, and I must have put them down somewhere, but I can't remember."

Their search of the small garden was fruitless, and the two knew there was only one course of action - call in Young Fred, their superhero.

"Don't worry, sister, Young Fred will find them, he's a good lad," said Emily, so Young Fred was sent for, and he turned up with his father, Fred senior, who, as he so often did, burst into tuneless song.

After two verses of 'The Wild Rover', Fred senior and Young Fred started their search, and soon found something in a nettle patch that made them start.

"Not the remains of an old boyfriend, is it, girls?" said Fred senior as he pulled the nettles off a collection of tiny bones.

"That's where they've ended up then, sister, I'll be blowed," said Emily, and told the two Freds: "That's the two kittens that died last year. We buried the little sweethearts behind the shed, but I reckon the old fox must have dug them up and dragged them here."

She explained that a fox, which they had christened Mr Foxy, visited the garden most nights, attracted to the kitchen scraps they left outside.

"I reckon he's taken a liking to more than your dinner. Looks like he's had a hankering for your teeth as well, Edith," said Fred senior, picking up a less than sparkling set of dentures.

"What's that black on them?" asked young Fred, as Fred senior dropped them into his hand. "That's fox crap, black and smelly," replied his father.

"On second thoughts," said Emily after giving Edith's prize teeth a close inspection, "I might give the old dentist a miss."

"Let me have those, please, Fred, I feel naked without them," said Edith, who walked back indoors clutching her unsavoury-looking dentures, black with fox poo

Young Fred followed her to the door to check she was okay, then stopped dead in his tracks, and turned back with a look of sheer amazement on his face.

"I don't believe what I've just seen," he whispered to his father. "She went indoors, gave her teeth a quick rub with a dirty old dish cloth, and put them straight back in her mouth; she never even washed them."

"She never does," said Emily, "Sister says it wears the enamel off."

Chapter 26

The Beach

"Are we all ready for our bit of fishing, then?" asked Sid of his darts team mates strung along the King's Head public bar.

"How are we getting there?" asked Dennis, pushing his empty glass across the polished top of the bar. "Another pint in there, please, Peggy love, and a bag of scratchings."

"We're taking my old van, Young Fred's driving," said Sid. "Does he know? It means he can't drink. I'm not sure he'll be too happy," said Norman, resplendent in thick fisherman's guernsey and wellington boots.

It was agreed among the four fishermen that Young Fred was the ideal choice to drive, as he drank less than they did. When he walked into the bar, laden down with fishing tackle, sandwich box and Thermos, they broke the news as gently as they could.

"We've elected you as driver, so only have one pint before we go," said Sid, who turned to Peggy and instructed: "Don't let him have more than one tonight, Peggy love, but he'll be okay on Coke."

"I think I've been stitched up here," said a bewildered Young Fred. "Did you know about this, dad?" Fred senior spluttered a bit, then changed the subject to check that someone had remembered to bring along the bait.

"Don't worry about that, just remember to bring me back a nice fat salmon, and don't you go falling in," said Peggy, who laughed as Fred senior confided that there were no salmon where they were going. "I know that, you daft sod. I know the nearest I'll get to a nice piece of salmon is if I go into the fishmonger in Malbury."

As the evening ended with Peggy's familiar "Haven't you got homes to go to, you lucky lads?" the five intrepid anglers filed out into the car park, Young Fred perfectly sober and the other four swaying and stumbling as Sid had half a dozen attempts to unlock his van before he miraculously found the keyhole.

Sid climbed into the passenger seat next to Young Fred, while the other three did their best to climb into the back without injury, although Dennis unfortunately failed on that score, and bruised both shins and cut his hand when he failed to notice the pile of fishing tackle which Fred senior was trying to load. At that point, Fred senior had also fallen over and was having difficulty getting back on his feet – it was a case of one step forward, two steps back, as the effects of too many pints of Old Todger took their toll.

"Oh no, what the heck's this?" coughed Norman, as he fell out of the rear doors of the van, looking like a snowman. "I should have told you," said Sid, "I dropped a bag of plaster and it split open. Sorry about that."

Eventually all five anglers and their equipment were inside the van, and Young Fred set off the five miles from Little Bardon to the short stretch of beach reached via the track to Great Wick Farm.

Young Fred was worried about driving on to the beach, but Sid assured him that he had done it many times in the old Land Rover he had a few years ago, and anyway they needed the van near at hand so they could brew up on his camping stove.

The short journey was uneventful, except for Dennis and Norman complaining about Fred senior's tuneless singing, and the whole party objecting to the after-effects of the six pickled eggs Dennis had eaten during the course of the evening in the pub.

With the van parked on the beach, and the fishing tackle unloaded, the planned all-night session could begin, but there was a little delay, although not one to really worry too much about, when Norman went to relieve himself, fell over and needed the other four to help him back to his very unsteady feet.

The fishing went well, albeit without catching anything worth keeping, and with a few tangled lines accompanied by expletives, but the intrepid anglers realised at about 3am that the tide was coming in at a fairly alarming rate, and they would have to make a move, especially as it had started to rain heavily.

So it was back to the van, for yet another brew-up, sitting listening to the rain beating on the roof and exchanging tales of the fish that were almost caught.

"I don't want to worry you," said Norman after returning from yet another trip to relieve himself, "but the tide's right up to the wheels. We need to go."

But that was easier said than done. Young Fred turned the key and nothing happened; Sid and Fred senior flipped the bonnet and hit the battery terminals with a lump of wood, and the van started, but by now it was sitting in nearly a foot of water and all efforts to drive out ended with spinning wheels and curses.

"Right lads, out and push," said Sid, and Dennis, Norman and Fred senior joined him to push the van out – except they couldn't. However hard they tried, the van was stuck fast and wouldn't move, and the tide was now coming in so fast it would soon swamp the engine.

Stumbling around in the dark, Dennis fell flat on his face in the cold water, Norman trod in a hole and ended with a wellington boot full of water, and Sid went into panic mode at the thought that the van he needed for work on Monday was going to be ruined by the rising water.

"Do you need our help?" came a voice out of the darkness. It was Waggy and Podge, the village's two enthusiastic poachers. "We certainly do," said Sid, "but what are you two doing out here? You're a long way from home."

"We're on one of our nature walks," said Waggy, putting down his bag of rabbit snares. "There's a new gamekeeper over at the estate and he's a bit keen, so we're keeping out of his way until he settles in and starts going to bed at night instead of being out looking for us."

With their help, the van was freed from the sand, and they headed back to the main road, where they were greeted by the flashing blue lights of Pc Nicholls' Ford Focus, and Young Fred was met by Pc Nicholls holding a breathalyser.

"That's all okay, but I need a look in the back. Can't be too careful at this time of the morning."

He opened the back doors and it was like a scene from a horror movie – Norman, Dennis and Fred senior were all white, covered head to foot in spilled plaster which had stuck to their wet clothes and started to harden.

"I'm lost for words. I've seen some strange sights in the early hours, but this one takes a bit of beating," said the chuckling policeman.

Fortunately he didn't look too closely at the contents of the van, so didn't see the bag of dead pheasants that Sid had promised to drop off at Waggy's back door.

Young Fred dropped three plaster-coated passengers in the village near the cemetery, which was handy for Norman as he needed to pop behind the cemetery wall for another pee.

The five had agreed to relive their fishing trip with a few Sunday lunchtime pints in the King's Head, where Peggy greeted them with: "Come on then, where's my fish?" Between them they spluttered half a dozen excuses for their lack of success, from the weather being against them to over-fishing by foreign trawlers.

"Is it five pints and five bags of scratchings, then, lads? And by the way, it seems you missed all the fun. Apparently that Mrs Nixon-Smith was driving home in the early hours from some fancy do and reckons she saw three zombies coming out of the cemetery. The woman's as daft as a brush."

Chapter 27

The Beano

There are occasions in every man's life that simply cannot be missed, they are so important that they take priority over everything else, such as his wedding, the birth of his first-born and, sadly, his funeral.

For those happy faces who frequent the public bar at the King's Head in Little Bardon, there is something far more important, infinitely more unmissable, than any of those - the annual beano.

The second Saturday in July means only one thing every year, that unmissable trip to Great Yarmouth, where sea air, greasy kebabs and copious amounts of beer make up a heady cocktail.

There is a rumour that on one occasion a beano-goer returned home sober and without throwing up at least once, but it is just a rumour, and one that has never been substantiated.

There are other rumours about the annual King's Head beano, including one said to involve pub regular and beano organiser Dennis, trouserless, and carrying a blow-up unicorn, being interviewed by police looking for a streaker.

Barmaid Peggy once said: "Who knows what barmy, drunken antics these daft sods are going to get up to when they're let off the leash once a year. All I can say, is Heaven help Great Yarmouth."

"Right lads, who's on the beano this year? Twenty quid for the coach. I need your names by Friday," Dennis announced on darts night.

Friday night came round and there was a spare seat. "Anyone know who we can get to fill the seat?" asked Dennis.

There were a few unwelcome suggestions and one or two rather lewd ones, then Joe piped up that old Mr Barrett had said that he would love a day out in Yarmouth, but definitely without the drinking. The problem was that octogenarian Mr Barrett, who lived in the old people's bungalows in the village, was renowned for his extreme flatulence.

"As long as I don't have to sit directly behind him, I say let him come with us," said Dennis, and so Mr Barrett's name was added to the beano list.

"I don't drink, except for a sherry at Christmas and a small Dubonnet on special occasions," Mr Barrett told Dennis when he arrived at the King's Head on the morning of the beano. "I have always wanted to go to Great Yarmouth for a day out and to bring home some bloaters. I am really excited, thank you for letting me join you."

"What on earth's a bloater?" asked Young Fred, who was waiting to get on the coach. Mr Barrett explained that it was a smoked herring, and his mother always served bloaters and brown bread for Saturday tea when he was a lad, and, he confided in a whisper, he had not tasted a bloater for more than 70 years.

"Right lads, if everyone is here, we'll get moving. Yarmouth, here we come, hold on to your women and get your beer pumps ready for action," shouted Dennis, to cheers and catcalls from the length of the coach.

It was an uneventful journey, except that Waggy and Podge, who were taking a day off from their usual Saturday fishing expeditions, had consumed 24 cans of lager between them before the coach reached the Norfolk border, and needed two unscheduled pee-break stops.

Next stop was Great Yarmouth's Golden Mile, which was reached with whoops and cheers from the thirsty beano crowd desperate to get started on the list of nine bars on the Great Yarmouth Ale Trail.

"And it's a minimum of a pint in each, boys," said Young Fred, as he led the way to the first pub. Waggy and Podge struggled to keep up, and actually struggled to even walk in a straight line, and Mr Barrett told everyone he wouldn't be drinking because he wanted to find the best bloaters.

"Just have one with us to get the day started, then you can go on your bloater hunt," said Dennis. "Just a small sherry then," said Mr Barrett, who eventually agreed to try a small whisky instead.

By the fourth pub, Mr Barrett, who said they should cut the formalities and call him Oswald, was extremely unsteady on his feet, thanks to countless small whiskies, and so were Waggy and Podge, who were conducting conversations with each other in a series of slurred and shouted words and half-finished sentences.

After pub number five the group agreed to have a break from drinking and to visit one of the town's two piers to find out who was the best dodgem car driver and to see if Fred senior really had his bragged-about sure-fire method to win on fruit machines.

Mr Barrett, Oswald, had to be supported by Sid and Joe, who were none too steady themselves, and Waggy and Podge decided that instead of the pier they would have forty winks on the beach until the serious drinking started again.

Young Fred and his mates Mark and Jason decided that now was a good time for a paddle, and Mr Barrett, by now what could best be described as whiffy, reminded those helping to keep him upright that he needed to find some bloaters.

This is what a beano is all about, thought Dennis, who prided himself on organising the best day out of the year. But his thoughts were interrupted by shouts from the water's edge, and the sight of Young Fred emerging from the waves soaked from head to toe.

Mark and Jason thought it hilarious, until the two of them fell backwards into the water, and Mark trod on Jason's glasses as they stumbled out, leaving sodden Jason struggling with the cumulative effects of extremely poor eyesight and beer haze.

After the pier, and Fred senior telling everyone the fruit machines must have been 'got at' for him to not win a jackpot even once, the group staggered on to the next pub, except for Waggy and Podge, who were still sound asleep on the beach, although Podge had woken once to be violently ill.

Sorry-looking and dripping wet, Young Fred, Mark and Jason trudged along behind, with a warning from Dennis that they may not be allowed into the pub in their soggy state.

Mr Barrett was still trying to find his bloaters, albeit in an incoherent way, and Waggy and Podge had now disappeared from the beach.

It was then that the singing started, led by tuneless Fred senior with his favourite 'The Wild Rover', but, after one verse and a chorus, the enthusiasm dried up and it was just Fred senior staggering along and bellowing his lungs out. He took great exception when an elderly woman confronted him and said: "Do you really have to? Leave singing to those who can." She pointed her walking stick at him and then disappeared with some head shaking and tut-tutting.

He was mortified. Him, Fred the singer, spoken to like that by a woman who had the audacity to question his fine singing voice. Fortunately for everyone around, the slight was enough to shut him up.

As afternoon turned to evening, and everyone was full of fish and chips, kebabs and pickled eggs, and after Dennis had dispatched Young Fred to buy bin bags for him, Mark and Jason to sit on for the coach ride home, Mr Barrett finally had to admit that he wasn't going to get his bloaters. "Maybe next year," Dennis told him.

Not surprisingly, after umpteen whiskies, he could barely say bloater, let alone go looking for them, but he knew the words of 'The Wild Rover', and suddenly burst into song, much to the delight of Fred senior, who joined in.

Then octogenarian Mr Barrett started to tap dance. "Stop him, someone," mumbled Dennis, the most coherent of the group. "He's going to end up going home in an ambulance if he carries on like that."

But the singing carried on, and the dancing carried on until Mr Barrett fell over and had to be helped back to his feet and on to the waiting coach by equally drunk assistants.

Waggy and Podge were nowhere to be found, and Waggy wasn't answering his mobile, so the drunken consensus was that they would have to spend a night in Yarmouth, rather than in their own beds. Dennis had fallen asleep, so it was left to Sid to marshal everyone on to the coach, including Young Fred, who appeared with bin bags under one arm and the other arm holding up paralytic John Boy, who lived in Little Bardon with his mum.

"I didn't even know you were on the beano," Young Fred told him. "I reckon you must have been sitting down the front of the bus."

The journey home was mostly quiet and subdued, the silence only broken by occasional snores, Mr Barrett's noisy flatulence and Fred senior breaking into 'The Wild Rover', only to be shouted at from all corners of the coach.

"Help me get John Boy off the coach, he's virtually unconscious," said Young Fred to Mark and Jason. "His mum's not going to be happy."

After much ringing and knocking, John Boy's elderly mum came to the door in her dressing gown, and looked aghast at Young Fred standing there holding up her very drunk son.

"What's he doing here? He's supposed to be on holiday with his sister in Yarmouth."

Next day, the beano-goers slunk silently into the King's Head one by one for their usual Sunday lunchtime pints, met by a smiling Peggy behind the bar, who asked Dennis: "Good beano, was it, Dennis? Did you all get blind drunk and make fools of yourselves?"

"No, very quiet, nothing to report, really. I think I'd better have a pint and a bag of scratchings, and have you got any aspirin, please, Peggy love?"

Chapter 28

Cor, That's A Lovely Drop

There is nothing to beat a nice pint of Old Todger in the public bar of the King's Head in Little Bardon, where barmaid Peggy expertly dispenses the amber nectar to her faithful regulars.

"Cor, that's a lovely drop, Peggy love," they tell her as they down that first refreshing pint in the early evening, accompanied, of course, by a bag of pork scratchings.

Looks of absolute contentment spread across the faces ranged along the bar as they enjoy that first pint, the one that leaves a little bit of foam on the top lip as it slides down so easily.

"Who could ever want more than this?" asked Norman, in reflective mood on darts night. "A pint, a bag of scratchings, and your smiling face the other side of the bar, Peggy love. You can keep your fancy cocktails and poncey pub grub. This is all a man needs."

There were grunts of approval along the bar, and a few moments of silence as the darts team, to a man, savoured their first pints. Then Young Fred piped up with: "That's all very well, Norman, but it's getting a bit pricey now that Old Todger is going up by ten pence a pint next week."

"Who's told you that?" asked Norman. "It's in today's local paper. Ten pence on a pint, true as I'm standing here," said Young Fred.

The news sent a shock wave through the darts team, and a declaration from Dennis, after some head-scratching calculations, "That's going to cost me another three or four quid a week."

"Is it true, Peggy love, ten pence on a pint? That's robbery. Us old boys can't afford that, we have problems enough with your prices now," said visibly disgruntled Norman.

"They're not my prices, Norman, the brewery is putting up its prices and so the pub is having to follow suit," replied Peggy.

"I think I'll start making my own," said Young Fred. "It can't be that hard. I made ginger beer a few years ago, and that was all right."

There were some doubts among the assembled company of beer afficionados about Young Fred's ability to produce any sort of beer, let alone a brew really worth drinking.

"Right, you're on, Young Fred," said Dennis. "We'll chip in a couple of quid each to buy whatever you need, and let you get on with it. You are now the darts team's official head brewer."

"You lot get barmier," said Peggy. "Letting Young Fred loose with your money and expecting him to produce something that's drinkable, it's a recipe for disaster. In the meantime, who's ready for another pint?"

She didn't have to ask twice, as the darts players are always ready for another pint, and so the evening continued, with pints drunk, darts thrown and Young Fred deep in thought about the challenge he had taken on.

"How's the beer going?" asked Dennis a few days later. "It's coming on nicely, ready to bottle in a couple of weeks, and will be drinkable in six," said Young Fred, keen to share his brewing prowess.

"I've been drinking a lot of cola, so I can save the two-litre bottles for the beer. I think you'll all be pleased with the results. I may turn this into a business, Little Bardon's own micro brewery. But I don't know what to call it."

"What about Fred's Folly or Barmy Bitter?" suggested Peggy, but they were suggestions that didn't go down well with Young Fred, who thought Fred's Brewery and Fred's Special Bitter sounded better.

I'M NOT ONE TO GOSSIP

Over the next few weeks, drinking in the public bar of the King's Head became almost a game of cat and mouse for the regulars who, as soon as Young Fred appeared, moved along the bar in a usually unsuccessful effort to shut out his incessant chatter about his beer making, and about the brewing empire that inevitably would follow.

"Do you have to keep on and on about your beer-making? You're driving my customers away. Just let them get on with enjoying their pints of proper beer," Peggy told him.

"Not jealous that Fred's Special Bitter is going to be better than Old Todger, are you, Peggy love? Do you know, I really think this could be the start of something big, huge in fact. You'll soon want to sell Fred's Special Bitter here. And who knows, I could follow it up with a lager – Fred's Lager – and even a special Christmas beer, and perhaps a chocolate-flavoured Easter beer."

"Learn to walk before you start running. We haven't tasted the first brew yet, and we might not like it," said Dennis.

Young Fred looked quite hurt at the suggestion that his beer might not have the taste that Little Bardon's bitter drinkers would enjoy.

"You'll all love it. I've put a lot of love and care into my first brew, to make it really special. I can't wait for you all to get your first taste."

It was decided that Sunday afternoon in a couple of weeks time would be the time to christen the brew. "A few pints in the pub first, then all round to my house to enjoy Fred's Special Bitter, and I'll get in a few bags of scratchings to make it like the pub."

"I'll bring along a few pickled eggs," said Norman. "That'll make it a proper session."

When Sunday came, there was a buzz in the public bar of the King's Head, at the thought of an afternoon drinking session without having to pay pub prices.

"I'm looking forward to this," said Joe to his brother Sid, as they desperately tried to stop Fred senior – Young Fred's dad - start his tuneless rendering of 'The Wild Rover', as they staggered past the village green under the watchful eye of Pc Nicholls, sitting enjoying a late lunch of a tuna baguette in his patrol car.

"I like your sign, boy, very good," Fred senior told his son as he, Sid and Joe staggered through the front door, past FREDS' BEWERY scrawled in garish lime green and pink felt tip on a pillow case pinned to the door, "but I'm not sure your mother is going to be too happy, and you need to brush up on your spelling."

The beer was in a dozen plastic bottles on the table, and the general consensus was that it looked as bitter should, with a nice amber colour and no cloudiness.

"Right, let's give it a try then, Young Fred, I'm sure we're all ready to sink a pint or two to put it to the test, especially as we've got scratchings and pickled eggs as well, just like a professional tasting session," said Dennis.

He admitted that he wasn't sure if they actually had pickled eggs and scratchings at professional tasting sessions, but that was definitely the Little Bardon way.

Young Fred poured the long-awaited fluid into a selection of glasses and mugs, raising his own Malbury Beer Festival 1998 glass as everyone downed their first taste of Fred's Special Bitter, amid spluttering, coughing and cries of "Young Fred, this is foul", "This is disgusting" and "Are you trying to poison us?"

The beer was sickly sweet and, to hardened bitter drinkers, completely undrinkable. "I can't understand it, I did everything it told me to when I read about it. I put in the right amount of malt extract and sugar, added the yeast, and let it stand for the right amount of time."

"How many dried hops did you put in to make it bitter, and take away the sweetness?" asked Dennis.

Young Fred displayed a familiar blank look. "Hops? I didn't know you had to put in hops."

"Reading was never the boy's strong point," said a disappointed Fred senior, staring into an empty glass.

Chapter 29

She's Behind You

"So it's agreed then, ladies, our pantomime this year will be Aladdin, performed in our very special Little Bardon Women's Institute way, with great talent and passion," announced an obviously over-excited Mrs Gladman to the WI's monthly meeting.

"The village hall will come alive with music and song and wonderful colourful costumes. I really can't wait."

"And who do you think she'll expect to make all those colourful costumes? Joe Muggins here, just because I can use a sewing machine," Mrs Barnes whispered to Mrs Ferguson.

"Just one moment, madam chairman," interjected Mrs Nixon-Smith, she of the big house, posh 4x4 and unruly spaniels, "who is going to direct this production? Without wishing to push myself forward, I must divulge that I have had considerable experience of treading the boards, as it were, and of taking the director's chair, when I lived in Surbiton. Much bigger productions, of course, and veritable magnets for talent scouts."

"Thank you, Mrs Nixon-Smith, that has been duly noted, but nothing has been decided yet. I will get back to you, as they say in showbusiness," replied Mrs Gladman, with a smirk that said I know, but I am not telling you.

"Another disaster in the making, just like Dick Whittington and his missing cat last year and Snow White three years ago," said Mrs Barnes to Mrs Gill as they walked home from the meeting.

"It was embarrassing for Snow White to only have four dwarves and for them to have to keep changing costumes to make it look like there were seven," chipped in a laughing Mrs Ferguson. "But at least the audience thought it was hilarious to see those poor children running about like idiots."

Mrs Gladman was in full pantomime mode at the next WI meeting. "I have the script and full list of characters, and I have put names to all of the main characters, except for the children, who Miss Day has offered to organise, as always. Right ladies, we must press on, chop chop."

"Don't you mean chopsticks?" asked Mrs Barnes, to a ripple of laughter. "You know full well that I don't mean chopsticks. Aladdin features a Chinese laundry, not a Chinese takeaway. Now let us move on to casting.

"Miss Smith, I was very impressed with your Snow White, so have cast you as Aladdin. Mrs Nixon-Smith, I think you will make a very good Wishee Washee, Aladdin's brother."

"Aladdin's simple-minded brother, you mean," said a very disgruntled Mrs Nixon-Smith, to which Mrs Barnes whispered that it was definitely type-casting. "I am not happy. I have played big, important roles in past productions in Surbiton. It was said that my Maria in The Sound of Music was a tour de force."

"Let us move on," said an exasperated Mrs Gladman, consulting her clipboard. "Mrs Ferguson, I would like you to play Widow Twanky, a very important role, and one that will show off your true abilities."

"She's very good with a washing machine," said Mrs Gill, to which Mrs Gladman informed her that the only skill Widow Twanky needed was in the use of a washboard.

"Iris, my dear, you will make an exceptionally good genie of the lamp, I am sure, and our new member, Mrs Burton, I would like to try you out as the Chinese emperor. There will of course, be a number of other roles - both on stage and behind the scenes - to be decided, and a piece of good news is that the two Freds, father and son, have agreed to construct and paint the scenery.

"Fred senior has also kindly offered to add his considerable vocal talents where needed, although I can't agree to his preferred song, which I believe is called 'The Wild Rover', even though he says he will learn to sing it in Chinese if required."

Even as Mrs Gladman was speaking, Young Fred was beavering away in his bedroom, drawing designs for the backdrop and making a list of the items needed on stage.

"Don't you think you should wait until old Gladman tells us what she wants?" asked Fred senior of his son. "That drawing is very nice, but I don't think she'll really want Aladdin prancing about in front of a picture of a railway station."

"No dad, that's the Taj Mahal. I've spent a couple of hours on the design. Do you like it?" said Young Fred. "Son, geography has never been your strong point. The Taj Mahal is in India, not China." A crestfallen Young Fred looked close to tears.

Pantomime rehearsals began a few weeks later with a read-through of the script, which threw up a few problems, such as Mrs Burton insisting on adopting a Chinese accent so extreme and absurd that no-one could understand a word she said.

"No, no, no, Mrs Burton, that will never do, that is not what we want," said a tetchy Mrs Gladman, at which Mrs Burton peeled off her home-made droopy moustache and declared that she was done with pantomime, and someone else could have the pleasure of playing the Chinese emperor.

"Very well, if that's how you feel. And Mrs Gill, Abanazar has to look menacing. He is seeking the magic lamp, not the packet of chocolate digestives that you are holding."

"But Mrs Gladman, I am having to pretend that the biscuits are the lamp, because Fred and Fred haven't made it yet," said Mrs Gill, who decided that if she couldn't pretend the biscuits were the lamp, she would open the packet and start eating them.

"Yes we have, it's here," said Fred senior, walking into the hall carrying an object made out of a small watering can covered in tinfoil.

"Do you not think it's perhaps a bit, umm, large?" asked Mrs Gladman, "but thank you, I am sure it will suffice."

"If Mrs Gill can lift it," whispered Mrs Barnes to Mrs Ferguson.

Rehearsals gathered pace, albeit with countless problems and with Mrs Gladman constantly holding her head in her hands and appearing to be on the verge of tears.

Mrs Ferguson couldn't remember her lines, Iris the postwoman couldn't stop laughing every time she made an appearance as the genie, and it was difficult to convince Mrs Nixon-Smith that Wishee Washee wasn't the central character.

"Mrs Nixon-Smith, please don't keep appearing on stage every time Aladdin starts speaking. I believe the theatrical phrase is please don't hog the limelight," said a now doubly-exasperated Mrs Gladman.

"Will you all just take note of instructions from the director, which is myself, of course, and not make your entrance until you see me raise my clipboard."

Excitement and anticipation grew as the opening night approached, with Fred senior still trying to convince Mrs Gladman that she should let him sing, and Young Fred working hard to complete the highly coloured backdrop, on the village hall stage, but disaster struck when he tripped and went headfirst through the canvas.

With just an hour to curtain up, he managed to repair the top-to-bottom tear with a large roll of sticky tape, but then had to repaint part of it, which is when he put his foot on an open paint pot and painted part of the stage a lovely shade of orange.

"I can't do this, dad, I can't do this," said Young Fred, as Fred senior did his best to help clean up, knocking over a tin of red paint in the process.

"Ten minutes to curtain up," called out Mrs Gladman, with a wave of her clipboard from the wings. "Miss Day, are the children ready? Mrs Nixon-Smith, you are not in the opening scene, so please stand back. Mrs Ferguson, where is your washboard?"

Mrs Barnes, still making last-minute adjustments to some costumes, couldn't suppress a laugh, although she was still unsure of her lines after being drafted in to replace Mrs Burton as the Chinese emperor, and was having problems with her droopy moustache falling off.

The music started, the audience clapped, and Miss Day's troupe of children danced across the stage, but disaster struck in the form of a slippery patch of red paint which caught a nine-year-old unawares and ended with her being helped off the floor with red paint over one side of the costume so lovingly crafted by Mrs Barnes.

The audience loved it, and thought it was all rehearsed, but Mrs Gladman was close to being distraught, and more so when Aladdin appeared for a solo singing spot, but Wishee Washee insisted on making it a duet. "Not yet, Wishee Washee, not yet. Please leave the stage," called out Mrs Gladman from the wings. "I haven't raised my clipboard yet."

The audience, between shouts of "She's behind you", could hear every instruction relayed by Mrs Gladman's booming voice, and were enjoying every minute of what was fast turning into a Keystone Kops comedy, with lines forgotten, Mrs Nixon-Smith popping out from the wings every few minutes, only to be called back by Mrs Gladman, and some dreadful, tuneless singing by everyone except the children.

"If she'd just let me sing, I could have saved this fiasco," Fred senior whispered to Iris, waiting to make her appearance as the genie. "Can you help me lift the magic lamp, Fred, it's a bit heavy," said Iris.

"I told the boy we should have used a lightweight plastic watering can rather than this metal one," replied Fred senior, between snatches of 'The Wild Rover' offstage, much to the annoyance of Mrs Gladman. "Please, no singing," she implored.

Chaos continued to reign until the final curtain, when Mrs Ferguson tripped and brought down Young Fred's carefully repaired backdrop onto the heads of Aladdin and Wishee Washee.

The audience loved it, thinking it was all part of the show, and only stopped clapping when Major Dobson, chairman of the parish council, got on to the stage and announced, in what some in the audience thought was a slightly inebriated voice: "Wonderful, wonderful, wonderful, Mrs Gladman and company. The funniest thing I have seen since the Morecambe and Wise Christmas show."

"Thank you, Mr Chairman, I did my best to inject a little humour," said a beaming Mrs Gladman, treading red footprints across the stage, as she hustled Mrs Nixon-Smith from centre stage to the wings.

"I told you you should have let me sing," said Fred senior, as Mrs Gladman left the stage

"Next year, Fred, next year."

Chapter 30

Let's Have A Party

"Listen up, boys, I've got an important announcement, and it involves all you lot in the darts team," Peggy shouted over the Friday night din in the King's Head's public bar between refilling glasses with innumerable pints of Old Todger.

"I know, I know," said Dennis, "You're running away with the vicar to start a new life as missionaries in Africa."

"Thank you, Dennis, now are there any more bright suggestions before I tell you? No, then listen. We're going to have a Christmas party, which will also celebrate Charlie's fifth Christmas as landlord here in Little Bardon."

"And my 21st birthday," said Young Fred. "Are you sure? You act as if you're only about ten?" laughed Norman, to catcalls from the rest of the darts team.

A sudden burst of enthusiasm filled the bar, even though it was two months until Christmas. It was quickly decided to host a children's party in the afternoon and a full-blown boozy do in the evening.

The enthusiasm did rather wane, though, when Fred senior said he would be delighted to sing; there were groans when he broke into his familiar off-key version of 'The Wild Rover', with Sid declaring that it would be one night when he turned his hearing aid off.

"We'll need to work out who to invite," said Peggy, "and will have to include the vicar and his fiancée, of course,"

"His bit of fluff, you mean, Peggy love," said Norman. "No, I don't. That is very rude. I hardly think a lady of her years could be described as a bit of fluff. She is going to marry the vicar, and a very nice lady she is too."

"Still his bit of fluff," chortled Norman, who quickly shut up when Peggy's withering look told him he had overstepped the mark.

"I would also like to invite the woman on local radio who Charlie listens to every afternoon. Can't think of her name, but she's always rabbiting on about her dogs. Just don't let her sing, I would rather listen to Fred, and that really is saying something," laughed Peggy.

For some obscure reason best known only to him, tone-deaf Fred senior took that as a compliment, which he met with a beaming smile.

Young Fred was equally full of smiles, delighted to be told that he could celebrate his 21st birthday at the pub - and then dropped his totally unexpected bombshell: "I'll be bringing my girlfriend."

The bar went very quiet, as Sid and Joe said together: "Are you sure?" Young Fred had never seen with a girl and had never shown any interest in the opposite sex – as least, that was what everyone had thought.

Young Fred confided that his love interest was Molly, the young dancer with Malbury Morris, who he had met at the village's Mayday Festival earlier in the year, when she beat him in the Welly Wanging contest, and who he had been secretly dating for months.

"I think me and you need a little talk about this, son, just come over here where it's quiet," said a worried-looking Fred senior. "So that's where you've been disappearing to on your motorbike, when you've said you're going to your mate Jason's.

"Son, I think it's probably time now for me to talk to you about, well, you know, about, you know, the sort of, well, birds and bees. You see, you're a good looking young man and Molly is a good looking young woman, and, well, things can sometimes happen, so you must always be prepared for all eventualities," said Fred senior, red with embarrassment, as the bar quietened and everyone strained to listen.

"Don't worry, dad, we're adults, and we're in love," replied Young Fred as the bar erupted in cheers and clapping.

"Give the boy another pint, and a celebration bag of scratchings," said Dennis, slapping Young Fred on the back.

Over the next few weeks, party arrangements were made, and a few surprises planned. Retired teacher Miss Day said she would organise the children's party and Reggie Naylor agreed to harness his Shire horses Major and Tommy to his beautifully restored farm waggon and transport Father Christmas into the village during the afternoon. But no-one in the darts team wanted to be Father Christmas, worried that Santa duties might impose on valuable drinking time. Mr Barrett from the old people's bungalows said he would, but he was given a gentle no by Norman who feared that his renowned noisy flatulence might not be the best accompaniment for a children's party.

Then Waggy, the village's infamous poacher, stepped into the breach and said he had always fancied himself in a red suit and white beard. Fellow poacher Podge, who resembles a man mountain, agreed, under intense pressure, particularly from Peggy, to be an elf, although it was suggested, a little unkindly, that there weren't many elves almost six feet tall and weighing sixteen stone. "I don't care if I look a complete wally, I'm going to do it for the kids," he said with a grimace.

The WI ladies were recruited to organise the Santa and elf costumes. "I know I'll get the job of making them," said Mrs Barnes. "I sometimes wish I'd never bought that blasted sewing machine."

At their November meeting, chair Mrs Gladman told them: "Come now ladies, we must all do our bit for the village kiddies. Perhaps someone other than our expert seamstress Mrs Barnes would like to make the required costumes. Come on, ladies, chop chop." Unsurprisingly, there were no takers.

Reggie Naylor's horses and farm waggon trundled down Little Bardon's village street through a flurry of snow on party afternoon, with Santa waving and his unconvincing elf helper desperately trying to keep his eight inch-long ears in place.

"Can you get me a couple of pheasants for Boxing Day?" called out someone from the pavement. "And I'd like a brace as well, and a rabbit, if you can," said someone else.

"I hope you're not planning to visit my land to get them, Waggy," said Reggie with a look over his shoulder that told Waggy and Podge to definitely stay away from Great Wick Farm on their next poaching expedition and take what they describe as a 'nature walk' elsewhere.

Santa and the ungainly elf arrived at the pub in clip-clopping style, to be met by cold, but excited, children outside, who were delighted to see the horses, although one little boy was in tears because he was expecting reindeer, and not Shire horses taller than his dad.

Waggy and Podge were wonderful with the children, who all went home happy, clutching sweets and a present, although that one little boy needed reassurance that there would be reindeer next year.

The adult fun started at seven, in the bar colourfully decorated earlier in the day by Norman, Dennis and Fred senior, and with a huge, multi-coloured HAPY CRISTMAS banner painted by Young Fred. "I do wish that boy could learn to spell, he embarrasses me," said Fred senior, who was desperate to start singing into the microphone which Joe and Sid had done their best to hide from him.

All the darts team turned up, and so did Mr Barrett, a couple of the WI ladies and Conrad with the tricky eye, who was disappointed that Charlie had switched the fruit machine off for the evening. Young Fred beamed as he showed off young Molly, who was embarrassed, but secretly pleased, to be the centre of attention.

Late in the evening, when most people were definitely the worse for wear, full of alcohol and food, and still trying to stop Fred senior from finding the microphone, Charlie called for order so he could thank everyone for their unwavering custom during his nearly five years as landlord.

Then he called Peggy from behind the bar, and told everyone how he could never have run the pub without her.

"He's sounding a bit sentimental," said Dennis to Norman, who replied that it was creepy, rather then sentimental. "I've never known him to be soppy, before. Pathetic, I call it."

Then Charlie dropped to one knee, and said, through tears: "Peggy, we've been more than just friends now for nearly a year, and I would like to make you the landlady of the King's Head, rather than the barmaid. What do you say?"

Peggy burst into tears and said: "Yes, yes, you silly sod, I suppose you're asking me to marry me. I wondered how long it would take you to ask me. Now someone give Fred that microphone and let's get this party started."

Chapter 31

It's Just Not Cricket

"Anyone up for a game of cricket? The new bloke in the shop reckons we ought to have a village cricket club," proclaimed Young Fred to the darts team limbering up with their first Friday night pints of Old Todger in the King's Head.

"Not me, I played cricket at school, until I got hit in the whatsits, so never again," said Dennis, taking a sharp intake of breath as he remembered that painful experience. "I'll stick to darts."

Imran and Shilpa Zafar had taken over struggling Moss & Lumley's general store a few months before, renamed it The Minimarket, and revived its fortunes.

"Nice couple, but he's always talking about cricket when I go in there," said Peggy from behind the bar. "Apparently he was captain of a cricket club when they lived in the Midlands, but it's too far for him to go now for a game. He's cricket mad."

Little Bardon had once had a cricket team, Norman reminded them, but it folded years ago, due to falling membership. "Maybe ought to start it again. We could practise one or two nights a week, then pile in here afterwards for a good session. And while you're standing there, Peggy love, another pint and bag of scratchings, please."

Young Fred was unanimously elected to talk to Imran about it – just as the pub regulars chose Young Fred every time something required a little effort. "I'll come with you, boy, I'm quite partial to the

Bombay Mix they sell," said Young Fred's dad, Fred senior, the village's tuneless tenor, who broke into 'The Wild Rover' at every opportunity, although this evening's rendition was met with a chorus of "Shut up, Fred," "Oh no, not that" and "Belt up, you dozy pillock," from the length of the bar.

"Why can't you go and do it, then, dad? You always expect me to do everything. It's always 'Young Fred will do this, Young Fred will do that', and I'm fed up with it."

But, despite his protestations, Young Fred went to see Imran the next day, and found a man totally immersed in cricket.

"He's a really nice bloke, but doesn't talk about anything but cricket, it's cricket this, cricket that, and even their cat is called Zat, which apparently is short for Howzat," Young Fred reported back to the darts team. Then Fred senior piped up: "Tell 'em the rest, boy, and make 'em really jealous."

It seems that, while they had been talking to Imran, Shilpa had brought out bowls of homemade vegetable curry and vegetable samosas for them to try. "I didn't think I liked vegetables, until I tasted that," confided Young Fred, whose eyes glazed over as he thought about Shilpa's cooking.

"If it's that good, I might ask her if she'll make some for us to sell in the bar, and perhaps we could have a curry night," enthused Peggy.

There were nods of approval from the assembled drinkers – except for Dennis, who "don't hold with that foreign muck." But, as Fred senior told him, laughingly: "You're just a miserable git."

The first evening cricket practice on the village green went well. Imran supplied bat, stumps and a soft practice ball, Conrad with the tricky eye produced pads out of his loft and Dennis took along a cricket box which his gran had bought him after his painful schooldays experience, but which had never been used.

There was an enthusiastic turnout, including village newcomer and talented all-rounder Walter Arbuthnot, who had played for his school team many years ago, and Pc Nicholls, the village bobby, who proved to be a demon fast bowler.

Then there was Young Fred, who was so keen to really look like a cricketer that he turned out in a white jumper his mum had knitted for his dad years ago, which had stretched so much after multiple washes that it almost reached his knees, and Norman, the village vegetable king, who wore his old motorcycle helmet "just in case".

The best part, for many of them, was the post-cricket evening afterwards in the King's Head, where Peggy and Shilpa between them had organised food, although it was pitiful to hear the moans and groans from the walking wounded.

Brothers Joe and Sid were both complaining about their backs after bowling attempts, Conrad with the tricky eye had bent a finger back attempting a diving catch and Fred senior was limping after falling over the bat and twisting his ankle – and staunchly denying Dennis' goading that he was too old to play and was "just an awkward old sod."

"Look at you lot, you're like a load of old crocks, half of you look as if you're on your last legs," laughed Peggy, shaking her head as she looked them up and down. "Truth is, most of us ARE old crocks, Peggy love, although I'm not so sure about being on our last legs," Norman replied, grateful that his crash helmet had not been put to the test, and nor had Dennis' cricket box.

"Take no notice of that, I think you all did brilliantly, for a first practice," said Imran, sipping a lemonade. "It's been wonderful to see such enthusiasm for this great game. Some regular practices and a few more players and we might have the makings of a village team."

Over the next few weeks, new faces started turning up on practice nights, including Imran's 15-year-old son Rohan and a couple of his friends from school in Malbury who lived in the village. A bonus was the cricket net that Pc Nicholls had managed to acquire from somewhere.

The fledgeling team was going from strength to strength under Imran's enthusiastic leadership, and he joined in the after-practice sessions in the King's Head, although with lemonade and crisps rather than pints of Old Todger and bags of pork scratchings.

All was going well until the night Young Fred announced mid-pint: "Molly and a couple of her friends want to join the team."

The King's Head's public bar went deathly quiet, then Dennis broke the silence, with a long drawn-out "Whhhhat!!"

A shocked Fred senior was quick to follow up with: "Boy, you can't have women playing a man's game. It's not right. It's like me and you joining a netball team. It's not right."

There were nods of agreement along the bar, then Peggy stopped halfway through pulling yet another pint, and told the assembly: "That's just what I expected to hear from you lot. You're living in the past. Having some women in the team might liven up some of you decrepit lot. I might even have a go myself."

"Now that would be a sight worth seeing, Peggy love. I'd better have another pint and bag of scratchings while I think about that," said Sid. He thought for moment, then said: "Perhaps you're right, but it still don't seem proper to have women playing."

Peggy pushed Sid's pint across the bar, and said: "Is it that you lot are scared that women will be better cricketers than you, fitter, keener and generally just better all round?"

"And better looking," threw in Young Fred, keen to enrol Molly and her friends into the team. "You're not wrong there," retorted Peggy with a laugh.

At the next practice session, Molly turned up with her friends Sarah and Jenny, all three members of Malbury Morris and enthusiastic netballers, keen to show their skills at another sport.

Imran suggested that the three should first have a go at bowling, and Young Fred, keen to show off to Molly, said she could bowl to him, which she did, and clean-bowled him, much to the amazement of box-equipped Dennis, keeping wicket.

"I've seen some really fast bowlers on the telly, but she really is something else," said Fred senior, as a disgruntled Young Fred complained that he had been caught off-guard as he hadn't been looking.

Imran was delighted with all three of the young women, after Sarah demonstrated how polishing one side of the ball made it swing – "my dad showed me how to do that," she said – and Jenny showed the benefits of watching old videos of her hero, Australia's late captain, Shane Warne, who had been a master of spin bowling.

After their amazing bowling performances, the three admitted that they had all played cricket before, at school, and that Sarah's dad was a former county player.

"We love all sports, and cricket is great," said Molly, clutching glum-looking Young Fred's hand. "But I still say you wouldn't have bowled me out if I had been looking," he said.

"You never did know how to be a good loser, did you boy," laughed Fred senior.

"Cheer up, Young Fred, we have the makings of a good team here, I am so excited. I am a happy man," said beaming Imran as he helped pull the motorcycle helmet off of Norman's head – "It's tight because I need a haircut," confided Norman.

Dennis was happy that his box hadn't been put to the test, and Fred senior and Conrad with the tricky eye were both just pleased to have survived yet another rigorous exercise session.

But Sid and Joe were both looking downcast, and only brightened up when they were clutching pints in the King's Head.

"How did it go?" asked Peggy, as she pushed yet more pints across the bar. "Well, the girls did pretty well, and they're all nice girls," said Sid, "but I still don't think it's right to have women playing a man's game.

"It's just not cricket."

Chapter 32

An Unlikely Hero

Fred Glee had never asked for much in life, and had never really achieved very much; his only claim to fame was being Little Bardon's oldest inhabitant.

He had been born in the village, married at the Union Chapel in the village, although the marriage had only lasted a few years, gone off to do National Service, and returned to an industrious but unremarkable life working for old Bert Naylor at Great Wick Farm.

Fred had never taken much of an interest in village life, although he enjoyed a pint and game of cribbage in the King's Head on Friday nights, and never missed a monthly bingo session in the village hall.

"I'm happy doin' what I'm a doin'," he would tell anyone who asked, but few people did ask, because Fred was not the most outgoing of men, preferring his own company, and the pleasures of sitting in his little bungalow and watching soaps and nature programmes on the 52-inch tv that his sister Doreen had persuaded him to buy.

He was sitting in front of that treasured tv when Doreen found him on one of her regular Monday visits to deliver a clean set of clothes. A community first responder from Malbury beat the ambulance by half an hour, but there was nothing anyone could do; Fred had probably been dead for at least a day.

"He would have been 100 in a few weeks, and was so looking forward to a telegram from the King," Doreen told Pc Nicholls when he sat down with her to get some information for the coroner. "He was a lovely brother, a lot older than me, of course, and we shared everything, except what he did in Korea, and he would never talk about that."

She explained that Fred simply refused to say anything about his service in the Korean War, in the early 1950s, brushing aside any questions with a simple "I didn't do anything special, I was just one of a number." She knew he had been a Royal Marine Commando, but nothing more.

Pc Nicholls was intrigued. His own father had been a Commando, although a few years after Fred's time, and had been proud to wear the green beret. "If you find his service record or any other information about your brother, I would love to have a look," he told Doreen.

She had to clear Fred's rented bungalow, so a few days later started the sad task of looking through the battered suitcase full of paperwork and yellowing newspapers he had kept tucked away under his bed.

It was a real hotch potch: a page torn from the *Malbury and District Recorder* from 1996 with a picture of Fred holding the trophy he won for his beautiful dahlias at the Malbury Flower and Produce Show, a couple of national newspapers with headlines about the death of Winston Churchill, cuttings about the first Moon landing.

And underneath them an envelope marked 'medals' and a dog-eared notebook with pages of handwritten entries written by Fred in the spidery, mis-spelled scrawl that had been so familiar to Doreen from the notes he used to leave her around his little bungalow.

On the front it said 'My bloody war', and Doreen instinctively knew it wasn't something she wanted to read alone; although Fred had never spoken about his time in Korea, she had always known that even thinking about it had been painful for him; but he hadn't wanted to speak about it, so she had never pressed him.

Pc Nicholls told her that he would be happy to go through it with her, if that was what she wanted, but in her home at the other end of the village, rather than in the bungalow where Fred had passed so recently.

Doreen knew that Fred had been fighting the communists in Malaya in 1950 when the North Koreans, backed by Russia, invaded South Korea; she had been a young girl at the time, and only knew about the war from what she had read afterwards.

Although she knew that her big brother had been in Korea, she had no clue about what he did there, and when he came back he shared nothing except occasional black moods when he took himself off for long walks across the fields.

Doreen poured the tea and she and Pc Nicholls settled down with Fred's notebook. "Are you sure you want me to read it, rather than you?" asked the young policeman. "I can't read it," said Doreen, "I know it will make me cry."

The first few pages, in Fred's barely legible writing, described how he joined the Royal Marines and trained in Devon as a commando, building lifelong friendships and earning the coveted green beret.

He was sent to Malaya as part of 3 Commando Brigade, where he was part of the guerrilla war against communist terrorists.

Then, as part of 41 Independent Commando, he was deployed to Camp McGill in Japan for further training and familiarisation with the American weapons they would be carrying in Korea.

"We knew this would be big," Fred wrote, "and we were ready for it, but we had to leave our Bren guns behind and get used to American M19s, which I wasn't too happy with at first."

Then he described how he was part of the 63-man force taken to Korea on American transport submarine *USS Perch,* from where they launched daring night attacks on Korean rail and supply lines.

They operated in sub-zero temperatures, and Fred described the pain of frostbite, but it was nothing to the pain that was to come.

"Me and Basil joined up together, trained together in Devon and went off to Malaya together," wrote Fred in his scrawly hand.

"I never thought my best mate, the toughest, gentlest, nicest person I had ever known, would die in my arms, and there was nothing I could do for him. All I could do was tell him I loved him as a brother and would never forget him. I still think about him every day, and each day I ask why it was him and not me who caught that bullet."

"There's more," said Pc Nicholls, "but I think that's probably enough for today. Let's put the book away now, and perhaps look again after Fred's funeral."

After he placed the book back in the suitcase, he opened the envelope that had been under the papers, and pulled out two medals.

It took just two minutes on his phone to find out that they were the UN Service Medal for Korea and the Korea Medal, with a bronze oak leaf attached to its yellow and blue ribbon.

"Do you know what the oak leaf means?" he asked a puzzled-looking Doreen. "It means Fred was mentioned in despatches; it means your big brother was a hero."

"And he never spoke about it, he never told anyone about his war," she said between sobs. "If anyone ever asked, he just said he didn't do anything special, but everyone who went out there did something special, didn't they."

Fred had been one of 82,000 British forces serving in the Korean War, which lasted three years and cost 1,100 British and 37,000 American lives, PC Nicholls told her.

Doreen agreed that, after Fred's funeral, his notebook and medals could become part of the village's growing history archive. Pc Nicholls arranged for that to happen, and Doreen told him: "I am so pleased and so proud that dear Fred won't be forgotten. I would like future generations to know that he was a hero."

Two Sundays later the young policeman met Doreen as she left for church, and told her: "The Reverend Stollery and I have arranged something special for this morning."

There was a knot of chattering villagers outside the village hall, who parted silently to let Doreen through, so she could see the newly-erected plaque on the wall next to the front door.

She read the words through a flood of tears, and leaning heavily on Pc Nicholls' supportive arm: 'In memory of Fred Glee, 1924-2023, a true son of Little Bardon and a real hero. RIP'

Milton Keynes UK
Ingram Content Group UK Ltd.
UKHW020213161223
434414UK00012B/75